Star Rover House
Jack London Books

The Son of the Wolf

The Man with the Gash
(formerly titled - The God
of His Fathers)

Nam-Bok
(formerly titled - Children
of the Frost)

The Sea-Wolf

The Cruise of the Dazzler

The People of the Abyss

Tales of the Fish Patrol

Before Adam

The Game

War of the Classes

Moon-Face

Bātard
(formerly titled —
The Faith of Men)

———

Jack London in "The Aegis"
(Introduction by James
E. Sisson III)

Jack London First Editions
by James E. Sisson III and
Robert W. Martens

BÂTARD

AND OTHER STORIES

This Collection of Stories was originally
published as "The Faith of Men".

The still was ready _ _ _ "Go forth
to the chief men of the village."

BÂTARD

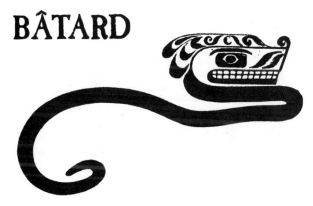

by

JACK LONDON

Star Rover House
Oakland, California
MCMLXXXVII

Contents

A RELIC OF THE PLIOCENE

A RELIC OF THE PLIOCENE

I WASH my hands of him at the start. I cannot father his tales, nor will I be responsible for them. I make these preliminary reservations, observe, as a guard upon my own integrity. I possess a certain definite position in a small way, also a wife; and for the good name of the community that honors my existence with its approval, and for the sake of her posterity and mine, I cannot take the chances I once did, nor foster probabilities with the careless improvidence of youth. So, I repeat, I wash my hands of him, this Nimrod, this mighty hunter, this homely, blue-eyed, freckle-faced Thomas Stevens.

Having been honest to myself, and to whatever prospective olive branches my wife may be pleased to tender me, I can now afford to

be generous.   I shall not criticise the tales
told me by Thomas Stevens, and, further, I
shall withhold my judgment.   If it be asked
why, I can only add that judgment I have
none.   Long have I pondered, weighed, and
balanced, but never have my conclusions been
twice the same — forsooth ! because Thomas
Stevens is a greater man than I.   If he have
told truths, well and good ; if untruths, still
well and good.   For who can prove ? or who
disprove ?   I eliminate myself from the propo-
sition, while those of little faith may do as I
have done — go find the said Thomas Stevens,
and discuss to his face the various matters which,
if fortune serve, I shall relate.   As to where
he may be found ?   The directions are simple :
anywhere between 53 north latitude and the
Pole, on the one hand ; and, on the other, the
likeliest hunting grounds that lie between
the east coast of Siberia and farthermost Labrador.   That he is there, somewhere, within
that clearly defined territory, I pledge the
word of an honorable man whose expecta-
tions entail straight speaking and right living.

Thomas Stevens may have toyed prodigiously with truth, but when we first met (it were well to mark this point), he wandered into my camp when I thought myself a thousand miles beyond the outermost post of civilization. At the sight of his human face, the first in weary months, I could have sprung forward and folded him in my arms (and I am not by any means a demonstrative man); but to him his visit seemed the most casual thing under the sun. He just strolled into the light of my camp, passed the time of day after the custom of men on beaten trails, threw my snowshoes the one way and a couple of dogs the other, and so made room for himself by the fire. Said he'd just dropped in to borrow a pinch of soda and to see if I had any decent tobacco. He plucked forth an ancient pipe, loaded it with painstaking care, and, without as much as by your leave, whacked half the tobacco of my pouch into his. Yes, the stuff was fairly good. He sighed with the contentment of the just, and literally absorbed the smoke from the crisping yellow flakes, and it did my smoker's heart good to behold him.

Hunter? Trapper? Prospector? He shrugged his shoulders No; just sort of knocking round a bit. Had come up from the Great Slave some time since, and was thinking of trapsing over into the Yukon country. The Factor of Koshim had spoken about the discoveries on the Klondike, and he was of a mind to run over for a peep. I noticed that he spoke of the Klondike in the archaic vernacular, calling it the Reindeer River — a conceited custom that the Old Timers employ against the *che-cha-quas* and all tenderfeet in general. But he did it so naïvely and as such a matter of course, that there was no sting, and I forgave him. He also had it in view, he said, before he crossed the divide into the Yukon, to make a little run up Fort o' Good Hope way.

Now Fort o' Good Hope is a far journey to the north, over and beyond the Circle, in a place where the feet of few men have trod; and when a nondescript ragamuffin comes in out of the night, from nowhere in particular, to sit by one's fire and discourse on such in terms of "trapsing" and "a little run," it is fair time to rouse up and shake off the dream. Wherefore I looked about me; saw the fly, and, underneath, the pine boughs spread for the sleeping furs; saw the grub sacks, the camera, the frosty breaths of the dogs circling on the edge of the light; and, above, a great streamer of the aurora bridging the zenith from southeast to northwest. I shivered. There is a magic in the Northland night, that steals in on one like fevers from malarial marshes. You are clutched and downed before you are aware. Then I looked to the snowshoes, lying prone and crossed where he had flung them. Also I had an eye to my tobacco pouch. Half, at least, of its goodly store had vamosed. That settled it. Fancy had not tricked me after all.

Crazed with suffering, I thought, looking steadfastly at the man — one of those wild stampeders, strayed far from his bearings and wandering like a lost soul through great vast-

nesses and unknown deeps. Oh, well, let his
moods slip on, until, mayhap, he gathers his
tangled wits together. Who knows? — the
mere sound of a fellow-creature's voice may
bring all straight again.

So I led him on in talk, and soon I marvelled, for he talked of game and the ways
thereof. He had killed the Siberian wolf of
westernmost Alaska, and the chamois in the
secret Rockies. He averred he knew the
haunts where the last buffalo still roamed;
that he had hung on the flanks of the caribou
when they ran by the hundred thousand, and
slept in the Great Barrens on the musk-ox's
winter trail.

And I shifted my judgment accordingly (the
first revision, but by no account the last), and
deemed him a monumental effigy of truth.
Why it was I know not, but the spirit moved
me to repeat a tale told to me by a man who
had dwelt in the land too long to know better.
It was of the great bear that hugs the steep
slopes of St. Elias, never descending to the
levels of the gentler inclines. Now God so

constituted this creature for its hillside habitat that the legs of one side are all of a foot longer than those of the other. This is mighty convenient, as will be readily admitted. So I hunted this rare beast in my own name, told it in the first person, present tense, painted the requisite locale, gave it the necessary garnishings and touches of verisimilitude, and looked to see the man stunned by the recital.

Not he. Had he doubted, I could have forgiven him. Had he objected, denying the dangers of such a hunt by virtue of the animal's inability to turn about and go the other way — had he done this, I say, I could have taken him by the hand for the true sportsman that he was. Not he. He sniffed, looked on me, and sniffed again; then gave my tobacco due praise, thrust one foot into my lap, and bade me examine the gear. It was a *mucluc* of the Innuit pattern, sewed together with sinew threads, and devoid of beads or furbelows. But it was the skin itself that was remarkable. In that it was all of half an inch thick, it reminded me of walrus-hide; but there the resemblance ceased, for no walrus ever bore so marvellous a growth of hair.   On the side and ankles this hair was well nigh worn away, what of friction with underbrush and snow; but around the top and down the more sheltered back it was coarse, dirty black, and very thick.   I parted it with difficulty and looked beneath for the fine fur that is common with northern animals, but found it in this case to be absent.   This, however, was compensated for by the length. Indeed, the tufts that had survived wear and tear measured all of seven or eight inches.

I looked up into the man's face, and he pulled his foot down and asked, "Find hide like that on your St. Elias bear?"

I shook my head.   "Nor on any other creature of land or sea," I answered candidly. The thickness of it, and the length of the hair, puzzled me.

"That," he said, and said without the slightest hint of impressiveness, "that came from a mammoth."

"Nonsense!" I exclaimed, for I could not

forbear the protest of my unbelief. "The mammoth, my dear sir, long ago vanished from the earth. We know it once existed by the fossil remains that we have unearthed, and by a frozen carcass that the Siberian sun saw fit to melt from out the bosom of a glacier; but we also know that no living specimen exists. Our explorers — "

At this word he broke in impatiently. "Your explorers? Pish! A weakly breed. Let us hear no more of them. But tell me, O man, what you may know of the mammoth and his ways."

Beyond contradiction, this was leading to a yarn; so I baited my hook by ransacking my memory for whatever data I possessed on the subject in hand. To begin with, I emphasized that the animal was prehistoric, and marshalled all my facts in support of this. I mentioned the Siberian sand bars that abounded with ancient mammoth bones; spoke of the large quantities of fossil ivory purchased from the Innuits by the Alaska Commercial Company; and acknowledged having myself mined six-

and eight-foot tusks from the pay gravel of the Klondike creeks. "All fossils," I concluded, "found in the midst of débris deposited through countless ages."

"I remember when I was a kid," Thomas Stevens sniffed (he had a most confounded way of sniffing), "that I saw a petrified watermelon. Hence, though mistaken persons sometimes delude themselves into thinking that they are really raising or eating them, there are no such things as extant water-melons."

"But the question of food," I objected, ignoring his point, which was puerile and without bearing. "The soil must bring forth vegetable life in lavish abundance to support so monstrous creations. Nowhere in the North is the soil so prolific. Ergo, the mammoth cannot exist."

"I pardon your ignorance concerning many matters of this Northland, for you are a young man and have travelled little; but, at the same time, I am inclined to agree with you on one thing. The mammoth no longer exists.

How do I know? I killed the last one with my own right arm."

Thus spake Nimrod, the Mighty Hunter. I threw a stick of firewood at the dogs and bade them quit their unholy howling, and waited. Undoubtedly this liar of singular felicity would open his mouth and requite me for my St. Elias bear.

"It was this way," he at last began, after the appropriate silence had intervened. "I was in camp one day — "

"Where?" I interrupted.

He waved his hand vaguely in the direction of the northeast, where stretched a terra incognita into which vastness few men have strayed and fewer emerged. "I was in camp one day with Klooch. Klooch was as handsome a little *kamooks* as ever whined betwixt the traces or shoved nose into a camp kettle. Her father was a full-blood Malemute from Russian Pastilik on Bering Sea, and I bred her, and with understanding, out of a clean-legged bitch of the Hudson Bay stock. I tell you, O man, she was a corker combination. And now, on

this day I have in mind, she was brought to
pup through a pure wild wolf of the woods —
gray, and long of limb, with big lungs and no
end of staying powers. Say! Was there ever
the like? It was a new breed of dog I had
started, and I could look forward to big things.

"As I have said, she was brought neatly to
pup, and safely delivered. I was squatting on
my hams over the litter — seven sturdy, blind
little beggars — when from behind came a bray
of trumpets and crash of brass. There was a
rush, like the wind-squall that kicks the
heels of the rain, and I was midway to my
feet when knocked flat on my face. At the
same instant I heard Klooch sigh, very much
as a man does when you've planted your fist
in his belly. You can stake your sack I lay
quiet, but I twisted my head around and saw
a huge bulk swaying above me. Then the
blue sky flashed into view and I got to my
feet. A hairy mountain of flesh was just dis-
appearing in the underbrush on the edge of
the open. I caught a rear-end glimpse, with
a stiff tail, as big in girth as my body, standing

out straight behind. The next second only a tremendous hole remained in the thicket, though I could still hear the sounds as of a tornado dying quickly away, underbrush ripping and tearing, and trees snapping and crashing.

" I cast about for my rifle. It had been lying on the ground with the muzzle against a log; but now the stock was smashed, the barrel out of line, and the working-gear in a thousand bits. Then I looked for the slut, and — and what do you suppose? "

I shook my head.

" May my soul burn in a thousand hells if there was anything left of her! Klooch, the seven sturdy, blind little beggars — gone, all gone. Where she had stretched was a slimy, bloody depression in the soft earth, all of a yard in diameter, and around the edges a few scattered hairs."

I measured three feet on the snow, threw about it a circle, and glanced at Nimrod.

" The beast was thirty long and twenty high," he answered, " and its tusks scaled over six times three feet. I couldn't believe, myself, at the time, for all that it had just happened. But if my senses had played me, there was the broken gun and the hole in the brush. And there was — or, rather, there was not — Klooch and the pups. O man, it makes me hot all over now when I think of it. Klooch! Another Eve! The mother of a new race! And a rampaging, ranting, old bull mammoth, like a second flood, wiping them, root and branch, off the face of the earth! Do you wonder that the blood-soaked earth cried out to high God? Or that I grabbed the hand-axe and took the trail?"

"The hand-axe?" I exclaimed, startled out of myself by the picture. "The hand-axe, and a big bull mammoth, thirty feet long, twenty feet — "

Nimrod joined me in my merriment, chuckling gleefully. "Wouldn't it kill you?" he cried. "Wasn't it a beaver's dream? Many's the time I've laughed about it since, but at the time it was no laughing matter, I was that danged mad, what of the gun and Klooch.

Think of it, O man! A brand-new, unclassified, uncopyrighted breed, and wiped out before ever it opened its eyes or took out its intention papers! Well, so be it. Life's full of disappointments, and rightly so. Meat is best after a famine, and a bed soft after a hard trail.

"As I was saying, I took out after the beast with the hand-axe, and hung to its heels down the valley; but when he circled back toward the head, I was left winded at the lower end. Speaking of grub, I might as well stop long enough to explain a couple of points. Up thereabouts, in the midst of the mountains, is an almighty curious formation. There is no end of little valleys, each like the other much as peas in a pod, and all neatly tucked away with straight, rocky walls rising on all sides. And at the lower ends are always small openings where the drainage or glaciers must have broken out. The only way in is through these mouths, and they are all small, and some smaller than others. As to grub — you've slushed around on the rain-soaked islands of the Alaskan coast down

Sitka way, most likely, seeing as you're a traveller. And you know how stuff grows there — big, and juicy, and jungly. Well, that's the way it was with those valleys. Thick, rich soil, with ferns and grasses and such things in patches higher than your head. Rain three days out of four during the summer months; and food in them for a thousand mammoths, to say nothing of small game for man.

"But to get back. Down at the lower end of the valley I got winded and gave over. I began to speculate, for when my wind left me my dander got hotter and hotter, and I knew I'd never know peace of mind till I dined on roasted mammoth-foot. And I knew, also, that that stood for *skookum mamook pukapuk* — excuse Chinook, I mean there was a big fight coming. Now the mouth of my valley was very narrow, and the walls steep. High up on one side was one of those big pivot rocks, or balancing rocks, as some call them, weighing all of a couple of hundred tons. Just the thing. I hit back for camp, keeping an eye open so the bull couldn't slip past, and got my ammunition. It wasn't worth anything with the rifle smashed; so I opened the shells, planted the powder under the rock, and touched it off with slow fuse. Wasn't much of a charge, but the old boulder tilted up lazily and dropped down into place, with just space enough to let the creek drain nicely. Now I had him."

"But how did you have him?" I queried. "Who ever heard of a man killing a mammoth with a hand-axe? And, for that matter, with anything else?"

"O man, have I not told you I was mad?" Nimrod replied, with a slight manifestation of sensitiveness. "Mad clean through, what of Klooch and the gun? Also, was I not a hunter? And was this not new and most unusual game? A hand-axe? Pish! I did not need it. Listen, and you shall hear of a hunt, such as might have happened in the youth of the world when caveman rounded up the kill with hand-axe of stone. Such would have served me as well. Now is it not a fact that man can outwalk the dog or horse? That he can wear them out with the intelligence of his endurance?"

I nodded.

"Well?"

The light broke in on me, and I bade him continue.

"My valley was perhaps five miles around. The mouth was closed. There was no way to get out. A timid beast was that bull mammoth, and I had him at my mercy. I got on his heels again, hollered like a fiend, pelted him with cobbles, and raced him around the valley three times before I knocked off for supper. Don't you see? A race-course! A man and a mammoth! A hippodrome, with sun, moon, and stars to referee!

"It took me two months to do it, but I did it. And that's no beaver dream. Round and round I ran him, me travelling on the inner circle, eating jerked meat and salmon berries on the run, and snatching winks of sleep between. Of course, he'd get desperate at times and turn. Then I'd head for soft

ground where the creek spread out, and lay
anathema upon him and his ancestry, and dare
him to come on.   But he was too wise to bog
in a mud puddle.   Once he pinned me in
against the walls, and I crawled back into
a deep crevice and waited.   Whenever he felt
for me with his trunk, I'd belt him with the
hand-axe till he pulled out, shrieking fit to
split my ear drums, he was that mad.   He
knew he had me and didn't have me, and it
near drove him wild.   But he was no man's
fool.   He knew he was safe as long as I stayed
in the crevice, and he made up his mind to
keep me there.   And he was dead right, only
he hadn't figured on the commissary.   There
was neither grub nor water around that spot,
so on the face of it he couldn't keep up
the siege.   He'd stand before the opening for
hours, keeping an eye on me and flapping
mosquitoes away with his big blanket ears.
Then the thirst would come on him and he'd
ramp round and roar till the earth shook, calling me every name he could lay tongue to.
This was to frighten me, of course; and when

he thought I was sufficiently impressed, he'd back away softly and try to make a sneak for the creek. Sometimes I'd let him get almost there — only a couple of hundred yards away it was — when out I'd pop and back he'd come, lumbering along like the old landslide he was. After I'd done this a few times, and he'd figured it out, he changed his tactics. Grasped the time element, you see. Without a word of warning, away he'd go, tearing for the water like mad, scheming to get there and back before I ran away. Finally, after cursing me most horribly, he raised the siege and deliberately stalked off to the water hole.

"That was the only time he penned me, — three days of it, — but after that the hippodrome never stopped. Round, and round, and round, like a six days' go-as-I-please, for he never pleased. My clothes went to rags and tatters, but I never stopped to mend, till at last I ran naked as a son of earth, with nothing but the old hand-axe in one hand and a cobble in the other. In fact, I never stopped, save for peeps of sleep in the crannies and ledges of the cliffs. As for the bull, he got perceptibly thinner and thinner — must have lost several tons at least — and as nervous as a schoolmarm on the wrong side of matrimony. When I'd come up with him and yell, or lam him with a rock at long range, he'd jump like a skittish colt and tremble all over. Then he'd pull out on the run, tail and trunk waving stiff, head over one shoulder and wicked eyes blazing, and the way he'd swear at me was something dreadful. A most immoral beast he was, a murderer, and a blasphemer.

" But toward the end he quit all this, and fell to whimpering and crying like a baby. His spirit broke and he became a quivering jelly-mountain of misery. He'd get attacks of palpitation of the heart, and stagger around like a drunken man, and fall down and bark his shins. And then he'd cry, but always on the run. O man, the gods themselves would have wept with him, and you yourself or any other man. It was pitiful, and there was so much of it, but I only hardened my heart and hit up the pace. At last I wore him clean out, and he lay down, broken-winded, broken-hearted, hungry, and thirsty. When I found he wouldn't budge, I hamstrung him, and spent the better part of the day wading into him with the hand-axe, he a sniffing and sobbing till I worked in far enough to shut him off. Thirty feet long he was, and twenty high, and a man could sling a hammock between his tusks and sleep comfortably. Barring the fact that I had run most of the juices out of him, he was fair eating, and his four feet, alone, roasted whole, would have lasted a man a twelvemonth. I spent the winter there myself."

"And where is this valley?" I asked.

He waved his hand in the direction of the northeast, and said: "Your tobacco is very good. I carry a fair share of it in my pouch, but I shall carry the recollection of it until I die. In token of my appreciation, and in return for the moccasins on your own feet, I will present to you these *muclucs*. They commemorate Klooch and the seven blind little beggars. They are also souvenirs of an unparalleled event in history, namely, the destruction of the oldest breed of animal on earth, and the youngest. And their chief virtue lies in that they will never wear out."

Having effected the exchange, he knocked the ashes from his pipe, gripped my hand good night, and wandered off through the snow. Concerning this tale, for which I have already disclaimed responsibility, I would recommend those of little faith to make a visit to the Smithsonian Institute. If they bring the requisite credentials and do not come in vacation time, they will undoubtedly gain an audience with Professor Dolvidson. The *muclucs* are in his possession, and he will verify, not the manner in which they were obtained, but the material of which they are composed. When he states that they are made from the skin of the mammoth, the scientific world accepts his verdict. What more would you have?

A HYPERBOREAN BREW

A HYPERBOREAN BREW

THE STORY OF A SCHEMING WHITE MAN AMONG
THE STRANGE PEOPLE WHO LIVE ON THE
RIM OF THE ARCTIC SEA

THOMAS STEVENS'S veracity may
have been indeterminate as x, and his
imagination the imagination of ordinary men increased to the nth power, but this,
at least, must be said: never did he deliver
himself of word nor deed that could be
branded as a lie outright. . . . He may have
played with probability, and verged on the
extremest edge of possibility, but in his tales
the machinery never creaked. That he knew
the Northland like a book, not a soul can
deny. That he was a great traveller, and had
set foot on countless unknown trails, many
evidences affirm. Outside of my own personal

knowledge, I knew men that had met him everywhere, but principally on the confines of Nowhere. There was Johnson, the ex-Hudson Bay Company factor, who had housed him in a Labrador factory until his dogs rested up a bit, and he was able to strike out again. There was McMahon, agent for the Alaska Commercial Company, who had run across him in Dutch Harbor, and later on, among the outlying islands of the Aleutian group. It was indisputable that he had guided one of the earlier United States surveys, and history states positively that in a similar capacity he served the Western Union when it attempted to put through its trans-Alaskan and Siberian telegraph to Europe. Further, there was Joe Lamson, the whaling captain, who, when ice-bound off the mouth of the Mackenzie, had had him come aboard after tobacco.

This last touch proves Thomas Stevens's identity conclusively. His quest for tobacco was perennial and untiring. Ere we became fairly acquainted, I learned to greet him with one hand, and pass the pouch with the other. But the night I met him in John O'Brien's Dawson saloon, his head was wreathed in a nimbus of fifty-cent cigar smoke, and instead of my pouch he demanded my sack. We were standing by a faro table, and forthwith he tossed it upon the " high card." "Fifty," he said, and the gamekeeper nodded. The "high card" turned, and he handed back my sack, called for a "tab," and drew me over to the scales, where the weigher nonchalantly cashed him out fifty dollars in dust.

" And now we'll drink," he said; and later, at the bar, when he lowered his glass: " Reminds me of a little brew I had up Tattarat way. No, you have no knowledge of the place, nor is it down on the charts. But it's up by the rim of the Arctic Sea, not so many hundred miles from the American line, and all of half a thousand God-forsaken souls live there, giving and taking in marriage, and starving and dying in-between-whiles. Explorers have overlooked them, and you will not find them in the census of 1890. A whale-ship was pinched there once, but the men, who had made shore over the ice, pulled out for the south and were never heard of.

"But it was a great brew we had, Moosu and I," he added a moment later, with just the slightest suspicion of a sigh.

I knew there were big deeds and wild doings behind that sigh, so I haled him into a corner, between a roulette outfit and a poker layout, and waited for his tongue to thaw.

"Had one objection to Moosu," he began, cocking his head meditatively — "one objection, and only one. He was an Indian from over on the edge of the Chippewyan country, but the trouble was, he'd picked up a smattering of the Scriptures. Been campmate a season with a renegade French Canadian who'd studied for the church. Moosu'd never seen applied Christianity, and his head was crammed with miracles, battles, and dispensations, and what not he didn't understand. Otherwise he was a good sort, and a handy man on trail or over a fire.

"We'd had a hard time together and were

badly knocked out when we plumped upon
Tattarat. Lost outfits and dogs crossing a
divide in a fall blizzard, and our bellies clove
to our backs and our clothes were in rags
when we crawled into the village. They
weren't much surprised at seeing us — because
of the whalemen — and gave us the meanest
shack in the village to live in, and the worst
of their leavings to live on. What struck me
at the time as strange was that they left us
strictly alone. But Moosu explained it.

"'Shaman *sick tumtum*,' he said, meaning
the shaman, or medicine man, was jealous,
and had advised the people to have nothing
to do with us. From the little he'd seen of
the whalemen, he'd learned that mine was a
stronger race, and a wiser; so he'd only
behaved as shamans have always behaved the
world over. And before I get done, you'll
see how near right he was.

"'These people have a law,' said Moosu:
'Whoso eats of meat must hunt. We be
awkward, you and I, O master, in the weap-
ons of this country; nor can we string bows

nor fling spears after the manner approved. Wherefore the shaman and Tummasook, who is chief, have put their heads together, and it has been decreed that we work with the women and children in dragging in the meat and tending the wants of the hunters.'

" 'And this is very wrong,' I made to answer; 'for we be better men, Moosu, than these people who walk in darkness. Further, we should rest and grow strong, for the way south is long, and on that trail the weak cannot prosper.'

" 'But we have nothing,' he objected, looking about him at the rotten timbers of the igloo, the stench of the ancient walrus meat that had been our supper disgusting his nostrils. 'And on this fare we cannot thrive. We have nothing save the bottle of "pain-killer," which will not fill emptiness, so we must bend to the yoke of the unbeliever and become hewers of wood and drawers of water. And there be good things in this place, the which we may not have. Ah, master, never has my nose lied to me, and I have followed it to secret caches and among the fur-bales of the igloos. Good provender did these people extort from the poor whalemen, and this provender has wandered into few hands. The woman Ipsukuk, who dwelleth in the far end of the village next the igloo of the chief, possesseth much flour and sugar, and even have my eyes told me of molasses smeared on her face. And in the igloo of Tummasook, the chief, there be tea — have I not seen the old pig guzzling? And the shaman owneth a caddy of "Star" and two buckets of prime smoking. And what have we? Nothing! Nothing! Nothing!'

" But I was stunned by the word he brought of the tobacco, and made no answer.

"And Moosu, what of his own desire, broke silence: 'And there be Tukeliketa, daughter of a big hunter and wealthy man. A likely girl. Indeed, a very nice girl.'

" I figured hard during the night while Moosu snored, for I could not bear the thought of the tobacco so near which I could not smoke. True, as he had said, we had nothing. But the way became clear to me, and in the morning I said to him: 'Go thou cunningly abroad, after thy fashion, and procure me some sort of bone, crooked like a gooseneck, and hollow. Also, walk humbly, but have eyes awake to the lay of pots and pans and cooking contrivances. And remember, mine is the white man's wisdom, and do what I have bid you, with sureness and despatch.'

"While he was away I placed the whale-oil cooking lamp in the middle of the igloo, and moved the mangy sleeping furs back that I might have room. Then I took apart his gun and put the barrel by handy, and afterward braided many wicks from the cotton that the women gather wild in the summer. When he came back, it was with the bone I had commanded, and with news that in the igloo of Tummasook there was a five-gallon kerosene can and a big copper kettle. So I said he had done well and we would tarry through the day. And when midnight was near I made harangue to him.

"'This chief, this Tummasook, hath a copper kettle, likewise a kerosene can.' I put a rock, smooth and wave-washed, in Moosu's hand. 'The camp is hushed and the stars are winking. Go thou, creep into the chief's igloo softly, and smite him thus upon the belly, and hard. And let the meat and good grub of the days to come put strength into thine arm. There will be uproar and outcry, and the village will come hot afoot. But be thou unafraid. Veil thy movements and lose thy form in the obscurity of the night and the confusion of men. And when the woman Ipsukuk is anigh thee, — she who smeareth her face with molasses, — do thou smite her likewise, and whosoever else that possesseth flour and cometh to thy hand. Then do thou lift thy voice in pain and double up with clasped hands, and make outcry in token that thou, too, hast felt the visitation of the night. And in this way shall we achieve honor and great possessions, and the caddy of "Star" and the prime smoking, and thy Tukeliketa, who is a likely maiden.'

"When he had departed on this errand, I bided patiently in the shack, and the tobacco seemed very near. Then there was a cry of affright in the night, that became an uproar and assailed the sky. I seized the 'pain-killer' and ran forth. There was much noise, and a wailing among the women, and fear sat heavily on all. Tummasook and the woman Ipsukuk rolled on the ground in pain, and with them there were divers others, also Moosu. I thrust aside those that cluttered the way of my feet, and put the mouth of the bottle to Moosu's lips. And straightway he became well and ceased his howling. Whereat there was a great clamor for the bottle from the others so stricken. But I made harangue, and ere they tasted and were made well I had mulcted Tummasook of his copper kettle and kerosene can, and the woman Ipsukuk of her sugar and molasses, and the other sick ones of goodly measures of flour. The shaman glowered wickedly at the people around my knees, though he poorly concealed the wonder that lay beneath. But I held my head high, and Moosu groaned beneath the loot as he followed my heels to the shack.

"There I set to work. In Tummasook's copper kettle I mixed three quarts of wheat flour with five of molasses, and to this I added of water twenty quarts. Then I placed the kettle near the lamp, that it might sour in the warmth and grow strong. Moosu understood, and said my wisdom passed understanding and was greater than Solomon's, who he had heard was a wise man of old time. The kerosene can I set over the lamp, and to its nose I affixed a snout, and into the snout the bone that was like a gooseneck. I sent Moosu without to pound ice, while I connected the barrel of his gun with the gooseneck, and midway on the barrel I piled the ice he had pounded. And at the far end of the gun barrel, beyond the pan of ice, I placed a small iron pot. When the brew was strong enough (and it was two days ere it could stand on its own legs), I filled the kerosene can with it, and lighted the wicks I had braided.

"Now that all was ready, I spoke to Moosu.

' Go forth,' I said, ' to the chief men of the village, and give them greeting, and bid them come into my igloo and sleep the night away with me and the gods.'

" The brew was singing merrily when they began shoving aside the skin flap and crawling in, and I was heaping cracked ice on the gun barrel. Out of the priming hole at the far end, drip, drip, drip into the iron pot fell the liquor — *hooch*, you know. But they'd never seen the like, and giggled nervously when I made harangue about its virtues. As I talked I noted the jealousy in the shaman's eye, so when I had done, I placed him side by side with Tummasook and the woman Ipsukuk. Then I gave them to drink, and their eyes watered and their stomachs warmed, till from being afraid they reached greedily for more ; and when I had them well started, I turned to the others. Tummasook made a brag about how he had once killed a polar bear, and in the vigor of his pantomime nearly slew his mother's brother. But nobody heeded. The woman Ipsukuk fell to weeping for a son lost

long years agone in the ice, and the shaman
made incantation and prophecy. So it went,
and before morning they were all on the floor,
sleeping soundly with the gods.

"The story tells itself, does it not? The
news of the magic potion spread. It was too
marvellous for utterance. Tongues could tell
but a tithe of the miracles it performed. It
eased pain, gave surcease to sorrow, brought
back old memories, dead faces, and forgotten
dreams. It was a fire that ate through all
the blood, and, burning, burned not. It
stoutened the heart, stiffened the back, and
made men more than men. It revealed the
future, and gave visions and prophecy. It
brimmed with wisdom and unfolded secrets.
There was no end of the things it could do,
and soon there was a clamoring on all hands
to sleep with the gods. They brought their
warmest furs, their strongest dogs, their best
meats ; but I sold the *hooch* with discretion,
and only those were favored that brought flour
and molasses and sugar. And such stores
poured in that I set Moosu to build a caché

to hold them, for there was soon no space in the igloo. Ere three days had passed Tummasook had gone bankrupt. The shaman, who was never more than half drunk after the first night, watched me closely and hung on for the better part of the week. But before ten days were gone even the woman Ipsukuk exhausted her provisions, and went home weak and tottery.

"But Moosu complained. 'O master,' he said, 'we have laid by great wealth in molasses and sugar and flour, but our shack is yet mean, our clothes thin, and our sleeping furs mangy. There is a call of the belly for meat the stench of which offends not the stars, and for tea such as Tummasook guzzles, and there is a great yearning for the tobacco of Neewak, who is shaman and who plans to destroy us. I have flour until I am sick, and sugar and molasses without stint, yet is the heart of Moosu sore and his bed empty.'

"'Peace!' I answered, 'thou art weak of understanding and a fool. Walk softly and wait, and we will grasp it all. But grasp now, and we grasp little, and in the end it will be nothing. Thou art a child in the way of the white man's wisdom. Hold thy tongue and watch, and I will show you the way my brothers do overseas, and, so doing, gather to themselves the riches of the earth. It is what is called "business," and what dost thou know about business?'

"But the next day he came in breathless. 'O master, a strange thing happeneth in the igloo of Neewak, the shaman; wherefore we are lost, and we have neither worn the warm furs nor tasted the good tobacco, what of your madness for the molasses and flour. Go thou and witness whilst I watch by the brew.'

"So I went to the igloo of Neewak. And behold, he had made his own still, fashioned cunningly after mine. And as he beheld me he could ill conceal his triumph. For he was a man of parts, and his sleep with the gods when in my igloo had not been sound.

"But I was not disturbed, for I knew what I knew, and when I returned to my own igloo, I descanted to Moosu and said: 'Happily the property right obtains amongst this people, who otherwise have been blessed with but few of the institutions of men. And because of this respect for property shall you and I wax fat, and, further, we shall introduce amongst them new institutions that other peoples have worked out through great travail and suffering.'

"But Moosu understood dimly, till the shaman came forth, with eyes flashing and a threatening note in his voice, and demanded to trade with me. 'For look you,' he cried, 'there be of flour and molasses none in all the village. The like have you gathered with a shrewd hand from my people, who have slept with your gods and who now have nothing save large heads, and weak knees, and a thirst for cold water that they cannot quench. This is not good, and my voice has power among them; so it were well that we trade, you and I, even as you have traded with them, for molasses and flour.'

"And I made answer: 'This be good talk, and wisdom abideth in thy mouth. We will trade. For this much of flour and molasses givest thou me the caddy of "Star" and the two buckets of smoking.'

"And Moosu groaned, and when the trade was made and the shaman departed, he upbraided me: 'Now, because of thy madness, are we, indeed, lost! Neewak maketh *hooch* on his own account, and when the time is ripe, he will command the people to drink of no *hooch* but his *hooch*. And in this way are we undone, and our goods worthless, and our igloo mean, and the bed of Moosu cold and empty!'

"And I answered: 'By the body of the wolf, say I, thou art a fool, and thy fathers before thee, and thy children after thee, down to the last generation. Thy wisdom is worse than no wisdom and thine eyes blinded to business, of which I have spoken and whereof thou knowest nothing. Go, thou son of a thousand fools, and drink of the *hooch* that Neewak brews in his igloo, and thank thy gods that thou hast a white man's wisdom to make soft the bed thou liest in. Go! and when thou hast drunken, return with the taste still on thy lips, that I may know.'

"And two days after, Neewak sent greeting and invitation to his igloo. Moosu went, but I sat alone, with the song of the still in my ears, and the air thick with the shaman's tobacco; for trade was slack that night, and no one dropped in but Angeit, a young hunter that had faith in me. Later, Moosu came back, his speech thick with chuckling and his eyes wrinkling with laughter.

"'Thou art a great man,' he said. 'Thou art a great man, O master, and because of thy greatness thou wilt not condemn Moosu, thy servant, who ofttimes doubts and cannot be made to understand.'

"'And wherefore now?' I demanded. 'Hast thou drunk overmuch? And are they sleeping sound in the igloo of Neewak, the shaman?'

"'Nay, they are angered and sore of body, and Chief Tummasook has thrust his thumbs in the throat of Neewak, and sworn by the bones of his ancestors to look upon his face

no more. For behold! I went to the igloo,
and the brew simmered and bubbled, and the
steam journeyed through the gooseneck even
as thy steam, and even as thine it became
water where it met the ice, and dropped into
the pot at the far end. And Neewak gave us
to drink, and lo, it was not like thine, for there
was no bite to the tongue nor tingling to the
eyeballs, and of a truth it was water. So we
drank, and we drank overmuch; yet did we
sit with cold hearts and solemn. And Neewak
was perplexed and a cloud came on his brow.
And he took Tummasook and Ipsukuk alone
of all the company and sat them apart, and
bade them drink and drink and drink. And
they drank and drank and drank, and yet sat
solemn and cold, till Tummasook arose in
wrath and demanded back the furs and the tea
he had paid. And Ipsukuk raised her voice,
thin and angry. And the company demanded
back what they had given, and there was a
great commotion.'

"'Does the son of a dog deem me a whale?'
demanded Tummasook, shoving back the skin

flap and standing erect, his face black and his brows angry.

"'Wherefore I am filled, like a fish-bladder, to bursting, till I can scarce walk, what of the weight within me? Lalah! I have drunken as never before, yet are my eyes clear, my knees strong, my hand steady.'

"'The shaman cannot send us to sleep with the gods,' the people complained, stringing in and joining us, 'and only in thy igloo may the thing be done.'

"So I laughed to myself as I passed the *hooch* around and the guests made merry. For in the flour I had traded to Neewak I had mixed much soda that I had got from the woman Ipsukuk. So how could his brew ferment when the soda kept it sweet? Or his *hooch* be *hooch* when it would not sour?

"After that our wealth flowed in without let or hindrance. Furs we had without number, and the fancy work of the women, all of the chief's tea, and no end of meat. One day Moosu retold for my benefit, and sadly mangled, the story of Joseph in Egypt, but from it I got an idea, and soon I had half the tribe at work building me great meat cachés. And of all they hunted I got the lion's share and stored it away. Nor was Moosu idle. He made himself a pack of cards from birch bark, and taught Neewak the way to play seven-up. He also inveigled the father of Tukeliketa into the game. And one day he married the maiden, and the next day he moved into the shaman's house, which was the finest in the village. The fall of Neewak was complete, for he lost all his possessions, his walrus-hide drums, his incantation tools — everything. And in the end he became a hewer of wood and drawer of water at the beck and call of Moosu. And Moosu — he set himself up as shaman, or high priest, and out of his garbled Scripture created new gods and made incantation before strange altars.

" And I was well pleased, for I thought it good that church and state go hand in hand, and I had certain plans of my own concerning the state. Events were shaping as I had foreseen. Good temper and smiling faces had vanished from the village. The people were morose and sullen. There were quarrels and fighting, and things were in an uproar night and day. Moosu's cards were duplicated and the hunters fell to gambling among themselves. Tummasook beat his wife horribly, and his mother's brother objected and smote him with a tusk of walrus till he cried aloud in the night and was shamed before the people. Also, amid such diversions no hunting was done, and famine fell upon the land. The nights were long and dark, and without meat no *hooch* could be bought; so they murmured against the chief. This I had played for, and when they were well and hungry, I summoned the whole village, made a great harangue, posed as patriarch, and fed the famishing. Moosu made harangue likewise, and because of this and the thing I had done I was made chief. Moosu, who had the ear of God and decreed his judgments, anointed me with whale blubber, and right blubberly he did it, not understanding the ceremony. And between us we interpreted to the people the new theory of the divine right of kings. There was *hooch* galore, and meat and feasting, and they took kindly to the new order.

"So you see, O man, I have sat in the high places, and worn the purple, and ruled populations. And I might yet be a king had the tobacco held out, or had Moosu been more fool and less knave. For he cast eyes upon Esanetuk, eldest daughter to Tummasook, and I objected.

"'O brother,' he explained, 'thou hast seen fit to speak of introducing new institutions amongst this people, and I have listened to thy words and gained wisdom thereby. Thou rulest by the God-given right, and by the God-given right I marry.'

"I noted that he 'brothered' me, and was angry and put my foot down. But he fell back upon the people and made incantations for three days, in which all hands joined; and then, speaking with the voice of God, he decreed polygamy by divine fiat. But he was shrewd, for he limited the number of wives by a property qualification, and because of which he, above all men, was favored by his wealth. Nor could I fail to admire, though it was plain that power had turned his head, and he would not be satisfied till all the power and all the wealth rested in his own hands. So he became swollen with pride, forgot it was I that had placed him there, and made preparations to destroy me.

"But it was interesting, for the beggar was working out in his own way an evolution of primitive society. Now I, by virtue of the *hooch* monopoly, drew a revenue in which I no longer permitted him to share. So he meditated for a while and evolved a system of ecclesiastical taxation. He laid tithes upon the people, harangued about fat firstlings and such things, and twisted whatever twisted texts he had ever heard to serve his purpose. Even this I bore in silence, but when he instituted what may be likened to a graduated income tax, I rebelled, and blindly, for this was what he worked for. Thereat, he appealed to the people, and they, envious of my great wealth and well taxed themselves, upheld him.

'Why should we pay,' they asked, 'and not you? Does not the voice of God speak through the lips of Moosu, the shaman?' So I yielded. But at the same time I raised the price of *hooch*, and lo, he was not a whit behind me in raising my taxes.

"Then there was open war. I made a play for Neewak and Tummasook, because of the traditionary rights they possessed; but Moosu won out by creating a priesthood and giving them both high office. The problem of authority presented itself to him, and he worked it out as it has often been worked before. There was my mistake. I should have been made shaman, and he chief; but I saw it too late, and in the clash of spiritual and temporal power I was bound to be worsted. A great controversy waged, but it quickly became one-sided. The people remembered that he had anointed me, and it was clear to them that the source of my authority lay, not in me, but in Moosu. Only a few faithful ones clung to me, chief among whom Angeit was; while he headed the popu-

lar party and set whispers afloat that I had it
in mind to overthrow him and set up my
own gods, which were most unrighteous gods.
And in this the clever rascal had anticipated
me, for it was just what I had intended —
forsake my kingship, you see, and fight spiritual with spiritual. So he frightened the people
with the iniquities of my peculiar gods — especially the one he named 'Biz-e-Nass' — and
nipped the scheme in the bud.

"Now, it happened that Kluktu, youngest
daughter to Tummasook, had caught my fancy,
and I likewise hers. So I made overtures,
but the ex-chief refused bluntly — after I had
paid the purchase price — and informed me
that she was set aside for Moosu. This was
too much, and I was half of a mind to go to his
igloo and slay him with my naked hands; but
I recollected that the tobacco was near gone,
and went home laughing. The next day he
made incantation, and distorted the miracle of
the loaves and fishes till it became prophecy,
and I, reading between the lines, saw that it
was aimed at the wealth of meat stored in

my cachés. The people also read between the lines, and, as he did not urge them to go on the hunt, they remained at home, and few caribou or bear were brought in.

"But I had plans of my own, seeing that not only the tobacco but the flour and molasses were near gone. And further, I felt it my duty to prove the white man's wisdom and bring sore distress to Moosu, who had waxed high-stomached, what of the power I had given him. So that night I went to my meat cachés and toiled mightily, and it was noted next day that all the dogs of the village were lazy. No one suspected, and I toiled thus every night, and the dogs grew fat and fatter, and the people lean and leaner. They grumbled and demanded the fulfilment of prophecy, but Moosu restrained them, waiting for their hunger to grow yet greater. Nor did he dream, to the very last, of the trick I had been playing on the empty cachés.

"When all was ready, I sent Angeit, and the faithful ones whom I had fed privily, through the village to call assembly. And the tribe gathered on a great space of beaten snow before my door, with the meat cachés towering stilt-legged in the rear. Moosu came also, standing on the inner edge of the circle opposite me, confident that I had some scheme afoot, and prepared at the first break to down me. But I arose, giving him salutation before all men.

"'O Moosu, thou blessed of God,' I began, 'doubtless thou hast wondered in that I have called this convocation together; and doubtless, because of my many foolishnesses, art thou prepared for rash sayings and rash doings. Not so. It has been said, that those the gods would destroy they first make mad. And I have been indeed mad. I have crossed thy will, and scoffed at thy authority, and done divers evil and wanton things. Wherefore, last night a vision was vouchsafed me, and I have seen the wickedness of my ways. And thou stoodst forth like a shining star, with brows aflame, and I knew in mine own heart thy greatness. I saw all things clearly. I knew that thou didst command the

ear of God, and that when you spoke he listened. And I remembered that whatever of
the good deeds that I had done, I had done
through the grace of God, and the grace of
Moosu.

"'Yes, my children,' I cried, turning to the
people, 'whatever right I have done, and
whatever good I have done, have been because
of the counsel of Moosu. When I listened
to him, affairs prospered; when I closed my
ears, and acted according to my folly, things
came to folly. By his advice it was that I laid
my store of meat, and in time of darkness fed
the famishing. By his grace it was that I
was made chief. And what have I done with
my chiefship? Let me tell you. I have
done nothing. My head was turned with
power, and I deemed myself greater than
Moosu, and, behold, I have come to grief.
My rule has been unwise, and the gods are
angered. Lo, ye are pinched with famine,
and the mothers are dry-breasted, and the
little babies cry through the long nights. Nor
do I, who have hardened my heart against

Moosu, know what shall be done, nor in what manner of way grub shall be had.'

"At this there was nodding and laughing, and the people put their heads together and I knew they whispered of the loaves and fishes. I went on hastily. 'So I was made aware of my foolishness and of Moosu's wisdom; of my own unfitness and of Moosu's fitness. And because of this, being no longer mad, I make acknowledgment and rectify evil. I did cast unrighteous eyes upon Kluktu, and lo, she was sealed to Moosu. Yet is she mine, for did I not pay to Tummasook the goods of purchase? But I am well unworthy of her, and she shall go from the igloo of her father to the igloo of Moosu. Can the moon shine in the sunshine? And further, Tummasook shall keep the goods of purchase, and she be a free gift to Moosu, whom God hath ordained her rightful lord.

"'And further yet, because I have used my wealth unwisely, and to oppress ye, O my children, do I make gifts of the kerosene can to Moosu, and the gooseneck, and the gun barrel, and the copper kettle. Therefore, I can gather to me no more possessions, and when ye are athirst for *hooch*, he will quench ye and without robbery. For he is a great man, and God speaketh through his lips.

"'And yet further, my heart is softened, and I have repented me of my madness. I, who am a fool and a son of fools; I, who am the slave of the bad god Biz-e-Nass; I, who see thy empty bellies and know not wherewith to fill them — why shall I be chief, and sit above thee, and rule to thine own destruction? Why should I do this, which is not good? But Moosu, who is shaman, and who is wise above men, is so made that he can rule with a soft hand and justly. And because of the things I have related do I make abdication and give my chiefship to Moosu, who alone knoweth how ye may be fed in this day when there be no meat in the land.'

"At this there was a great clapping of hands, and the people cried, '*Kloshe! Kloshe!*' which means, 'good.' I had seen the wonder-worry in Moosu's eyes; for he could not understand,

and was fearful of my white man's wisdom. I
had met his wishes all along the line, and even
anticipated some; and standing there, self-
shorn of all my power, he knew the time did
not favor to stir the people against me.

"Before they could disperse I made an-
nouncement that while the still went to Moosu,
whatever *hooch* I possessed went to the people. Moosu tried to protest at this, for never
had we permitted more than a handful to be
drunk at a time; but they cried, '*Kloshe!
Kloshe!*' and made festival before my door.
And while they waxed uproarious without, as
the liquor went to their heads, I held council
within with Angeit and the faithful ones. I
set them the tasks they were to do, and put
into their mouths the words they were to say.
Then I slipped away to a place back in the
woods where I had two sleds, well loaded, with
teams of dogs that were not overfed. Spring
was at hand, you see, and there was a crust to
the snow; so it was the best time to take the
way south. Moreover, the tobacco was gone.
There I waited, for I had nothing to fear.

Did they bestir themselves on my trail, their
dogs were too fat, and themselves too lean, to
overtake me; also, I deemed their bestirring
would be of an order for which I had made
due preparation.

"First came a faithful one, running, and
after him another. 'O master,' the first cried
breathless, 'there be great confusion in the
village, and no man knoweth his own mind,
and they be of many minds. Everybody hath
drunken overmuch, and some be stringing
bows, and some be quarrelling one with another. Never was there such a trouble.'

"And the second one: 'And I did as thou
biddest, O master, whispering shrewd words
in thirsty ears, and raising memories of the
things that were of old time. The woman
Ipsukuk waileth her poverty and the wealth
that no longer is hers. And Tummasook
thinketh himself once again chief, and the
people are hungry and rage up and down.'

"And a third one: 'And Neewak hath
overthrown the altars of Moosu, and maketh
incantation before the time-honored and an-

cient gods. And all the people remember the wealth that ran down their throats, and which they possess no more. And first, Esanetuk, who be *sick tumtum*, fought with Kluktu, and there was much noise. And next, being daughters of the one mother, did they fight with Tukeliketa. And after that did they three fall upon Moosu, like wind-squalls, from every hand, till he ran forth from the igloo, and the people mocked him. For a man who cannot command his womankind is a fool.'

"Then came Angeit: 'Great trouble hath befallen Moosu, O master, for I have whispered to advantage, till the people came to Moosu, saying they were hungry and demanding the fulfilment of prophecy. And there was a loud shout of "Itlwillie! Itlwillie!" (Meat.) So he cried peace to his womenfolk, who were overwrought with anger and with *hooch*, and led the tribe even to thy meat cachés. And he bade the men open them and be fed. And lo, the cachés were empty. There was no meat. They stood without sound, the people being frightened, and in the silence I lifted my voice. "O Moosu, where is the meat? That there was meat we know. Did we not hunt it and drag it in from the hunt? And it were a lie to say one man hath eaten it; yet have we seen nor hide nor hair. Where is the meat, O Moosu? Thou hast the ear of God. Where is the meat?"

"'And the people cried, "Thou hast the ear of God. Where is the meat?" And they put their heads together and were afraid. Then I went among them, speaking fearsomely of the unknown things, of the dead that come and go like shadows and do evil deeds, till they cried aloud in terror and gathered all together, like little children afraid of the dark. Neewak made harangue, laying this evil that had come upon them at the door of Moosu. When he had done, there was a furious commotion, and they took spears in their hands, and tusks of walrus, and clubs, and stones from the beach. But Moosu ran away home, and because he had not drunken of *hooch* they could not catch him, and fell one over another and made

haste slowly. Even now they do howl without his igloo, and his womanfolk within, and
what of the noise, he cannot make himself
heard.'

"'O Angeit, thou hast done well,' I com-
mended. 'Go now, taking this empty sled
and the lean dogs, and ride fast to the igloo
of Moosu; and before the people, who are
drunken, are aware, throw him quick upon
the sled and bring him to me.'

" I waited and gave good advice to the
faithful ones till Angeit returned. Moosu
was on the sled, and I saw by the fingermarks
on his face that his womankind had done well
by him. But he tumbled off and fell in the
snow at my feet, crying: 'O master, thou
wilt forgive Moosu, thy servant, for the
wrong things he has done! Thou art a great
man! Surely wilt thou forgive!'

"'Call me "brother," Moosu — call me
"brother,"' I chided, lifting him to his feet
with the toe of my moccasin. 'Wilt thou
evermore obey?'

"'Yea, master,' he whimpered, 'evermore.'

"'Then dispose thy body, so, across the sled.' I shifted the dogwhip to my right hand. 'And direct thy face downward, toward the snow. And make haste, for we journey south this day.' And when he was well fixed I laid the lash upon him, reciting, at every stroke, the wrongs he had done me. 'This, for thy disobedience in general — whack! And this for thy disobedience in particular — whack! whack! And this for Esanetuk! And this for thy soul's welfare! And this for the grace of thy authority! And this for Kluktu! And this for thy rights God-given! And this for thy fat firstlings! And this and this for thy income tax and thy loaves and fishes! And this for all thy disobedience! And this, finally, that thou mayest henceforth walk softly and with understanding! Now cease thy sniffling and get up! Gird on thy snowshoes and go to the fore and break trail for the dogs. *Chook! Mush-on!* Git!'"

Thomas Stevens smiled quietly to himself as he lighted his fifth cigar and sent curling smoke-rings ceilingward.

"But how about the people of Tattarat?" I asked. "Kind of rough, wasn't it, to leave them flat with famine?"

And he answered, laughing, between two smoke-rings, "Were there not the fat dogs?"

THE FAITH OF MEN

THE FAITH OF MEN

"TELL you what we'll do; we'll shake for it."

"That suits me," said the second man, turning, as he spoke, to the Indian that was mending snowshoes in a corner of the cabin. "Here, you Billebedam, take a run down to Oleson's cabin like a good fellow and tell him we want to borrow his dice box."

This sudden request in the midst of a council on wages of men, wood, and grub surprised Billebedam. Besides, it was early in the day, and he had never known white men of the caliber of Pentfield and Hutchinson to dice and play till the day's work was done. But his face was impassive as a Yukon Indian's should be, as he pulled on his mittens and went out the door.

Though eight o'clock, it was still dark outside, and the cabin was lighted by a tallow candle thrust into an empty whiskey bottle. It stood on the pine board table in the middle of a disarray of dirty tin dishes. Tallow from innumerable candles had dripped down the long neck of the bottle and hardened into a miniature glacier. The small room, which composed the entire cabin, was as badly littered as the table. While at one end, against the wall, were two bunks, one above the other, with the blankets turned down just as the two men had crawled out in the morning.

Lawrence Pentfield and Corry Hutchinson were millionnaires, though they did not look it. There seemed nothing unusual about them, while they would have passed muster as fair specimens of lumbermen in any Michigan camp. But outside, in the darkness, where holes yawned in the ground, were many men engaged in windlassing muck and gravel and gold from the bottoms of the holes where other men received fifteen dollars per day for scraping it from off the bedrock. Each day thousands of dollars' worth of gold were scraped from bedrock and windlassed to the surface, and it all belonged to Pentfield and Hutchinson, who took their rank among the richest kings of Bonanza.

Pentfield broke the silence that followed on Billebedam's departure by heaping the dirty plates higher on the table and drumming a tattoo on the cleared space with his knuckles. Hutchinson snuffed the smoky candle and reflectively rubbed the soot from the wick between thumb and forefinger.

"By Jove, I wish we could both go out!" he abruptly exclaimed. "That would settle it all."

Pentfield looked at him darkly.

"If it weren't for your cursed obstinacy, it'd be settled anyway. All you have to do is get up and get. I'll look after things, and next year I can go out."

"Why should I go? I've no one waiting for me—"

"Your people," Pentfield broke in roughly.

"Like you have," Hutchinson went on. "A girl, I mean, and you know it."

Pentfield shrugged his shoulders gloomily.

"She can wait, I guess."

"But she's been waiting two years now."

"And another won't age her beyond recognition."

"That'd be three years. Think of it, old man, three years in this end of the earth, this falling-off place for the damned!" Hutchinson threw up his arm in an almost articulate groan.

He was several years younger than his partner, not more than twenty-six, and there was a certain wistfulness in his face that comes into the faces of men when they yearn vainly for the things they have been long denied. This same wistfulness was in Pentfield's face, and the groan of it was articulate in the heave of his shoulders.

"I dreamed last night I was in Zinkand's," he said. "The music playing, glasses clinking, voices humming, women laughing, and I was ordering eggs — yes, sir, eggs, fried and boiled and poached and scrambled, and in all sorts of ways, and downing them as fast as they arrived."

"I'd have ordered salads and green things," Hutchinson criticised hungrily, "with a big, rare porterhouse, and young onions and radishes, the kind your teeth sink into with a crunch."

"I'd have followed the eggs with them, I guess, if I hadn't awakened," Pentfield replied.

He picked up a trail-scarred banjo from the floor and began to strum a few wandering notes. Hutchinson winced and breathed heavily.

"Quit it!" he burst out with sudden fury, as the other struck into a gayly lilting swing. "It drives me mad. I can't stand it."

Pentfield tossed the banjo into a bunk and quoted : —

" Hear me babble what the weakest won't confess —
      I am Memory and Torment — I am Town !
   I am all that ever went with evening dress !"

The other man winced where he sat and dropped his head forward on the table. Pentfield resumed the monotonous drumming with his knuckles. A loud snap from the door attracted his attention. The frost was creeping up the inside in a white sheet, and he began to hum : —

> " The flocks are folded, boughs are bare,
>   The salmon takes the sea ;
>   And oh, my fair, would I somewhere
>   Might house my heart with thee."

Silence fell and was not again broken till Billebedam arrived and threw the dice box on the table.

" Um much cold," he said. " Oleson um speak to me, um say um Yukon freeze last night."

" Hear that, old man ! " Pentfield cried, slapping Hutchinson on the shoulder. " Whoever wins can be hitting the trail for God's country this time to-morrow morning ! "

He picked up the box, briskly rattling the dice.

" What'll it be ? "

" Straight poker dice," Hutchinson answered. " Go on and roll them out."

Pentfield swept the dishes from the table with a crash, and rolled out the five dice. Both looked eagerly. The shake was without a pair and five-spot high.

"A stiff!" Pentfield groaned.

After much deliberating Pentfield picked up all the five dice and put them in the box.

"I'd shake to the five if I were you," Hutchinson suggested.

"No, you wouldn't, not when you see this," Pentfield replied, shaking out the dice.

Again they were without a pair, running this time in unbroken sequence from two to six.

"A second stiff!" he groaned. "No use your shaking, Corry. You can't lose."

The other man gathered up the dice without a word, rattled them, rolled them out on the table with a flourish, and saw that he had likewise shaken a six-high stiff.

"Tied you, anyway, but I'll have to do better than that," he said, gathering in four of them and shaking to the six. "And here's what beats you."

But they rolled out deuce, tray, four, and five, — a stiff still and no better nor worse than Pentfield's throw.

Hutchinson sighed.

"Couldn't happen once in a million times," he said.

"Nor in a million lives," Pentfield added, catching up the dice and quickly throwing them out. Three fives appeared, and, after much delay, he was rewarded by a fourth five on the second shake. Hutchinson seemed to have lost his last hope.

But three sixes turned up on his first shake. A great doubt rose in the other's eyes, and hope returned into his. He had one more shake. Another six and he would go over the ice to salt water and the states.

He rattled the dice in the box, made as though to cast them, hesitated, and continued to rattle them.

"Go on! Go on! Don't take all night about it!" Pentfield cried sharply, bending his nails on the table, so tight was the clutch with which he strove to control himself.

The dice rolled forth, an upturned six meeting their eyes. Both men sat staring at it. There was a long silence. Hutchinson shot a covert glance at his partner, who, still more covertly, caught it, and pursed up his lips in an attempt to advertise his unconcern.

Hutchinson laughed as he got up on his feet. It was a nervous, apprehensive laugh. It was a case where it was more awkward to win than lose. He walked over to his partner, who whirled upon him fiercely : —

" Now you just shut up, Corry ! I know all you're going to say — that you'd rather stay in and let me go, and all that; so don't say it. You've your own people in Detroit to see, and that's enough. Besides, you can do for me the very thing I expected to do if I went out."

" And that is — ? "

Pentfield read the full question in his partner's eyes, and answered : —

" Yes, that very thing. You can bring her in to me. The only difference will be a Dawson wedding instead of a San Franciscan one."

"But man alive!" Corry Hutchinson objected. "How under the sun can I bring her in? We're not exactly brother and sister, seeing that I have not even met her, and it wouldn't be just the proper thing, you know, for us to travel together. Of course, it would be all right — you and I know that; but think of the looks of it, man!"

Pentfield swore under his breath, consigning the looks of it to a less frigid region than Alaska.

"Now, if you'll just listen and not get astride that high horse of yours so blamed quick," his partner went on, "you'll see that the only fair thing under the circumstances is for me to let you go out this year. Next year is only a year away, and then I can take my fling."

Pentfield shook his head, though visibly swayed by the temptation.

"It won't do, Corry, old man. I appreciate your kindness and all that, but it won't do. I'd be ashamed every time I thought of you slaving away in here in my place."

A thought seemed suddenly to strike him. Burrowing into his bunk and disrupting it in his eagerness, he secured a writing pad and pencil, and sitting down at the table, began to write with swiftness and certitude.

"Here," he said, thrusting the scrawled letter into his partner's hand. "You just deliver that and everything'll be all right."

Hutchinson ran his eye over it and laid it down.

"How do you know the brother will be willing to make that beastly trip in here?" he demanded.

"Oh, he'll do it for me — and for his sister," Pentfield replied. "You see, he's tenderfoot, and I wouldn't trust her with him alone. But with you along it will be an easy trip and a safe one. As soon as you get out, you'll go to her and prepare her. Then you can take your run East to your own people, and in the spring she and her brother'll be ready to start with you. You'll like her, I know, right from the jump; and from that, you'll know her as soon as you lay eyes on her."

So saying he opened the back of his watch and exposed a girl's photograph pasted on the inside of the case. Corry Hutchinson gazed at it with admiration welling up in his eyes.

"Mabel is her name," Pentfield went on. "And it's just as well you should know how to find the house. Soon as you strike 'Frisco, take a cab and just say, 'Holmes's place, Myrdon Avenue' — I doubt if the Myrdon Avenue is necessary. The cabby'll know where Judge Holmes lives."

"And say," Pentfield continued, after a pause, "it won't be a bad idea for you to get me a few little things which — a — er — "

"A married man should have in his business," Hutchinson blurted out with a grin.

Pentfield grinned back.

"Sure, napkins and tablecloths and sheets and pillowslips, and such things. And you might get a good set of china. You know it'll come hard for her to settle down to this sort of thing. You can freight them in by steamer around by Bering Sea. And, I say, what's the matter with a piano?"

Hutchinson seconded the idea heartily. His reluctance had vanished, and he was warming up to his mission.

"By Jove! Lawrence," he said at the conclusion of the council, as they both rose to their feet, "I'll bring back that girl of yours in style. I'll do the cooking and take care of the dogs, and all that brother'll have to do will be to see to her comfort and do for her whatever I've forgotten. And I'll forget damn little, I can tell you."

The next day Lawrence Pentfield shook hands with him for the last time and watched him, running with his dogs, disappear up the frozen Yukon on his way to salt water and the world. Pentfield went back to his Bonanza mine, which was many times more dreary than before, and faced resolutely into the long winter. There was work to be done, men to superintend, and operations to direct in burrowing after the erratic pay streak; but his heart was not in the work. Nor was his heart in any work till the tiered logs of a new cabin began to rise on the hill behind the mine. It was a grand cabin, warmly built and divided into three comfortable rooms. Each log was hand-hewed and squared — an expensive whim when the axemen received a daily wage of fifteen dollars; but to him nothing could be too costly for the home in which Mabel Holmes was to live.

So he went about with the building of the cabin, singing, "And oh, my fair, would I somewhere might house my heart with thee!" Also, he had a calendar pinned on the wall above the table, and his first act each morning was to check off the day and to count the days that were left ere his partner would come booming down the Yukon ice in the spring. Another whim of his was to permit no one to sleep in the new cabin on the hill. It must be as fresh for her occupancy as the square-hewed wood was fresh; and when it stood complete, he put a padlock on the door. No one entered save himself, and he was wont to spend long hours there, and to come forth with his face strangely radiant and in his eyes a glad, warm light.

In December he received a letter from
Corry Hutchinson. He had just seen Mabel
Holmes. She was all she ought to be, to be
Lawrence Pentfield's wife, he wrote. He was
enthusiastic, and his letter sent the blood tingling through Pentfield's veins. Other letters
followed, one on the heels of another and
sometimes two or three together when the mail
lumped up. And they were all in the same
tenor. Corry had just come from Myrdon
Avenue; Corry was just going to Myrdon
Avenue; or Corry was at Myrdon Avenue.
And he lingered on and on in San Francisco,
nor even mentioned his trip to Detroit.

Lawrence Pentfield began to think that his
partner was a great deal in the company of
Mabel Holmes for a fellow who was going
East to see his people. He even caught himself worrying about it at times, though he
would have worried more had he not known
Mabel and Corry so well. Mabel's letters, on
the other hand, had a great deal to say about
Corry. Also, a thread of timidity that was
near to disinclination ran through them con-

cerning the trip in over the ice and the Dawson marriage. Pentfield wrote back heartily,
laughing at her fears, which he took to be the
mere physical ones of danger and hardship
rather than those bred of maidenly reserve.

But the long winter and tedious wait, following upon the two previous long winters, were
telling upon him. The superintendence of the
men and the pursuit of the pay streak could
not break the irk of the daily round, and the
end of January found him making occasional
trips to Dawson, where he could forget his
identity for a space at the gambling tables.
Because he could afford to lose, he won, and
" Pentfield's luck " became a stock phrase
among the faro players.

His luck ran with him till the second week
in February. How much farther it might
have run is conjectural; for, after one big
game, he never played again.

It was in the Opera House that it occurred,
and for an hour it had seemed that he could
not place his money on a card without making
the card a winner. In the lull at the end of a

deal, while the game keeper was shuffling the
deck, Nick Inwood, the owner of the game,
remarked, apropos of nothing : —

"I say, Pentfield, I see that partner of yours
has been cutting up monkeyshines on the
outside."

"Trust Corry to have a good time," Pentfield had answered; "especially when he has
earned it."

"Every man to his taste," Nick Inwood
laughed; "but I should scarcely call getting
married a good time."

"Corry married!" Pentfield cried, incredu-
lous and yet surprised out of himself for the
moment.

"Sure," Inwood said. "I saw it in the
'Frisco paper that came in over the ice this
morning."

"Well, and who's the girl?" Pentfield demanded, somewhat with the air of patient
fortitude with which one takes the bait of a
catch and is aware at the time of the large
laugh bound to follow at his expense.

Nick Inwood pulled the newspaper from

his pocket and began looking it over, saying : —

"I haven't a remarkable memory for names, but it seems to me it's something like Mabel — Mabel — oh, yes, here is it — 'Mabel Holmes, daughter of Judge Holmes, — whoever he is.'"

Lawrence Pentfield never turned a hair, though he wondered how any man in the North could know her name. He glanced coolly from face to face to note any vagrant signs of the game that was being played upon him, but beyond a healthy curiosity the faces betrayed nothing. Then he turned to the gambler and said in cold, even tones: —

"Inwood, I've got an even five hundred here that says the print of what you have just said is not in that paper."

The gambler looked at him in quizzical surprise.

"Go 'way, child. I don't want your money."

"I thought so," Pentfield sneered, returning to the game and laying a couple of bets.

Nick Inwood's face flushed, and, as though doubting his senses, he ran careful eyes over the print of a quarter of a column. Then he turned on Lawrence Pentfield.

"Look here, Pentfield," he said, in quick, nervous manner; "I can't allow that, you know."

"Allow what?" Pentfield demanded brutally.

"You implied that I lied."

"Nothing of the sort," came the reply. "I merely implied that you were trying to be clumsily witty."

"Make your bets, gentlemen," the dealer protested.

"But I tell you it's true," Nick Inwood insisted.

"And I have told you I've five hundred that says it's not in that paper," Pentfield answered, at the same time throwing a heavy sack of dust on the table.

"I am sorry to take your money," was the retort, as Inwood thrust the newspaper into Pentfield's hand.

Pentfield saw, though he could not quite bring himself to believe. Glancing through the headline, "Young Lochinvar came out of the North," and skimming the article until the names of Mabel Holmes and Corry Hutchinson, coupled together, leaped squarely before his eyes, he turned to the top of the page. It was a San Francisco paper.

"The money's yours, Inwood," he remarked, with a short laugh. "There's no telling what that partner of mine will do when he gets started."

Then he returned to the article and read it word for word, very slowly and very carefully. He could no longer doubt. Beyond dispute, Corry Hutchinson had married Mabel Holmes. "One of the Bonanza kings," it described him, "a partner with Lawrence Pentfield (whom San Francisco society has not yet forgotten), and interested with that gentleman in other rich Klondike properties." Further, and at the end, he read, "It is whispered that Mr. and Mrs. Hutchinson will, after a brief trip east to Detroit, make their real honeymoon journey into the fascinating Klondike country."

"I'll be back again; keep my place for me," Pentfield said, rising to his feet and taking his sack, which meantime had hit the blower and came back lighter by five hundred dollars.

He went down the street and bought a Seattle paper. It contained the same facts, though somewhat condensed. Corry and Mabel were indubitably married. Pentfield returned to the Opera House and resumed his seat in the game. He asked to have the limit removed.

"Trying to get action," Nick Inwood laughed, as he nodded assent to the dealer. "I was going down to the A. C. store, but now I guess I'll stay and watch you do your worst."

This Lawrence Pentfield did at the end of two hours' plunging, when the dealer bit the end off a fresh cigar and struck a match as he announced that the bank was broken. Pentfield cashed in for forty thousand, shook hands with Nick Inwood, and stated that it was the last time he would ever play at his game or at anybody else's.

No one knew nor guessed that he had been hit, much less hit hard. There was no apparent change in his manner. For a week he went about his work much as he had always done, when he read an account of the marriage in a Portland paper. Then he called in a friend to take charge of his mine and departed up the Yukon behind his dogs. He held to the Salt Water trail till White River was reached, into which he turned. Five days later he came upon a hunting camp of the White River Indians. In the evening there was a feast, and he sat in honor beside the chief; and next morning he headed his dogs back toward the Yukon. But he no longer travelled alone. A young squaw fed his dogs for him that night and helped to pitch camp. She had been mauled by a bear in her childhood and suffered from a slight limp. Her name was Lashka, and she was diffident at first with the strange white man that had come out of the Unknown, married her with scarcely a look or word, and now was carrying her back with him into the Unknown.

But Lashka's was better fortune than falls to most Indian girls that mate with white men in the Northland. No sooner was Dawson reached than the barbaric marriage that had joined them was resolemnized, in the white man's fashion, before a priest. From Dawson, which to her was all a marvel and a dream, she was taken directly to the Bonanza claim and installed in the square-hewed cabin on the hill.

The nine days' wonder that followed arose not so much out of the fact of the squaw whom Lawrence Pentfield had taken to bed and board as out of the ceremony that had legalized the tie. The properly sanctioned marriage was the one thing that passed the community's comprehension. But no one bothered Pentfield about it. So long as a man's vagaries did no special hurt to the community, the community let the man alone,

nor was Pentfield barred from the cabins of
men who possessed white wives. The marriage ceremony removed him from the status
of squaw-man and placed him beyond moral
reproach, though there were men that challenged his taste where women were concerned.

No more letters arrived from the outside.
Six sledloads of mail had been lost at the
Big Salmon. Besides, Pentfield knew that
Corry and his bride must by that time have
started in over the trail. They were even
then on their honeymoon trip — the honeymoon trip he had dreamed of for himself
through two dreary years. His lip curled
with bitterness at the thought; but beyond
being kinder to Lashka he gave no sign.

March had passed and April was nearing
its end, when, one spring morning, Lashka
asked permission to go down the creek several miles to Siwash Pete's cabin. Pete's
wife, a Stewart River woman, had sent up
word that something was wrong with her
baby, and Lashka, who was preëminently a
mother-woman and who held herself to be

truly wise in the matter of infantile troubles, missed no opportunity of nursing the children of other women as yet more fortunate than she.

Pentfield harnessed his dogs, and with Lashka behind took the trail down the creek bed of Bonanza. Spring was in the air. The sharpness had gone out of the bite of the frost, and though snow still covered the land, the murmur and trickling of water told that the iron grip of winter was relaxing. The bottom was dropping out of the trail, and here and there a new trail had been broken around open holes. At such a place, where there was not room for two sleds to pass, Pentfield heard the jingle of approaching bells and stopped his dogs.

A team of tired-looking dogs appeared around the narrow bend, followed by a heavily loaded sled. At the gee-pole was a man who steered in a manner familiar to Pentfield, and behind the sled walked two women. His glance returned to the man at the gee-pole. It was Corry. Pentfield got

on his feet and waited. He was glad that
Lashka was with him. The meeting could
not have come about better had it been
planned, he thought. And as he waited he
wondered what they would say, what they
would be able to say. As for himself there
was no need to say anything. The explain-
ing was all on their side, and he was ready
to listen to them.

As they drew in abreast, Corry recognized
him and halted the dogs. With a " Hello,
old man," he held out his hand.

Pentfield shook it, but without warmth or
speech. By this time the two women had
come up, and he noticed that the second one
was Dora Holmes. He doffed his fur cap,
the flaps of which were flying, shook hands
with her, and turned toward Mabel. She
swayed forward, splendid and radiant, but fal-
tered before his outstretched hand. He had
intended to say, " How do you do, Mrs. Hutchinson ? " — but somehow, the Mrs. Hutchinson had choked him, and all he had managed
to articulate was the " How do you do ? "

There was all the constraint and awkwardness in the situation he could have wished. Mabel betrayed the agitation appropriate to her position, while Dora, evidently brought along as some sort of peacemaker, was saying:—

"Why, what is the matter, Lawrence?"

Before he could answer, Corry plucked him by the sleeve and drew him aside.

"See here, old man, what's this mean?" Corry demanded in a low tone, indicating Lashka with his eyes.

"I can hardly see, Corry, where you can have any concern in the matter," Pentfield answered mockingly.

But Corry drove straight to the point.

"What is that squaw doing on your sled? A nasty job you've given me to explain all this away. I only hope it can be explained away. Who is she? Whose squaw is she?"

Then Lawrence Pentfield delivered his stroke, and he delivered it with a certain calm elation of spirit that seemed somewhat to compensate for the wrong that had been done him.

"She is my squaw," he said; "Mrs. Pentfield, if you please."

Corry Hutchinson gasped, and Pentfield left him and returned to the two women. Mabel, with a worried expression on her face, seemed holding herself aloof. He turned to Dora and asked, quite genially, as though all the world was sunshine: —

"How did you stand the trip, anyway? Have any trouble to sleep warm?"

"And how did Mrs. Hutchinson stand it?" he asked next, his eyes on Mabel.

"Oh, you dear ninny!" Dora cried, throwing her arms around him and hugging him. "Then you saw it, too! I thought something was the matter, you were acting so strangely."

"I — I hardly understand," he stammered.

"It was corrected in next day's paper," Dora chattered on. "We did not dream you would see it. All the other papers had it correctly, and of course that one miserable paper was the very one you saw!"

"Wait a moment! What do you mean?"

Pentfield demanded, a sudden fear at his heart, for he felt himself on the verge of a great gulf.

But Dora swept volubly on.

"Why, when it became known that Mabel and I were going to Klondike, *Every Other Week* said that when we were gone, it would be lovely on Myrdon Avenue, meaning, of course, lonely."

"Then—"

"I am Mrs. Hutchinson," Dora answered. "And you thought it was Mabel all the time."

"Precisely the way of it," Pentfield replied slowly. "But I can see now. The reporter got the names mixed. The Seattle and Portland papers copied."

He stood silently for a minute. Mabel's face was turned toward him again, and he could see the glow of expectancy in it. Corry was deeply interested in the ragged toe of one of his moccasins, while Dora was stealing sidelong glances at the immobile face of Lashka sitting on the sled. Lawrence Pentfield stared straight out before him into a dreary future, through the gray vistas of which he saw himself riding on a sled behind running dogs with lame Lashka by his side.

Then he spoke, quite simply, looking Mabel in the eyes.

"I am very sorry. I did not dream it. I thought you had married Corry. That is Mrs. Pentfield sitting on the sled over there."

Mabel Holmes turned weakly toward her sister, as though all the fatigue of her great journey had suddenly descended on her. Dora caught her around the waist. Corry Hutchinson was still occupied with his moccasins. Pentfield glanced quickly from face to face, then turned to his sled.

"Can't stop here all day, with Pete's baby waiting," he said to Lashka.

The long whip-lash hissed out, the dogs sprang against the breast bands, and the sled lurched and jerked ahead.

"Oh, I say, Corry," Pentfield called back, "you'd better occupy the old cabin. It's not been used for some time. I've built a new one on the hill."

TOO MUCH GOLD

TOO MUCH GOLD

THIS being a story — and a truer one than it may appear — of a mining country, it is quite to be expected that it will be a hard-luck story. But that depends on the point of view. Hard luck is a mild way of terming it so far as Kink Mitchell and Hootchinoo Bill are concerned; and that they have a decided opinion on the subject is a matter of common knowledge in the Yukon country.

It was in the fall of 1896 that the two partners came down to the east bank of the Yukon, and drew a Peterborough canoe from a moss-covered caché. They were not particularly pleasant-looking objects. A summer's prospecting, filled to repletion with hardship and rather empty of grub, had left their clothes in tatters and themselves worn and cadaverous. A nimbus of mosquitoes buzzed about each man's head. Their faces were coated with blue clay. Each carried a lump of this damp clay, and, whenever it dried and fell from their faces, more was daubed on in its place. There was a querulous plaint in their voices, an irritability of movement and gesture, that told of broken sleep and a losing struggle with the little winged pests.

"Them skeeters'll be the death of me yet," Kink Mitchell whimpered, as the canoe felt the current on her nose, and leaped out from the bank.

"Cheer up, cheer up. We're about done," Hootchinoo Bill answered, with an attempted heartiness in his funereal tones that was ghastly. "We'll be in Forty Mile in forty minutes, and then —cursed little devil!"

One hand left his paddle and landed on the back of his neck with a sharp slap. He put a fresh daub of clay on the injured part, swearing sulphurously the while. Kink Mitchell was not in the least amused. He merely improved the opportunity by putting a thicker coating of clay on his own neck.

They crossed the Yukon to its west bank, shot down-stream with easy stroke, and at the end of forty minutes swung in close to the left around the tail of an island. Forty Mile spread itself suddenly before them. Both men straightened their backs and gazed at the sight. They gazed long and carefully, drifting with the current, in their faces an expression of mingled surprise and consternation slowly gathering. Not a thread of smoke was rising from the hundreds of log-cabins. There was no sound of axes biting sharply into wood, of hammering and sawing. Neither dogs nor men loitered before the big store. No steamboats lay at the bank, no canoes, nor scows, nor poling-boats. The river was as bare of craft as the town was of life.

"Kind of looks like Gabriel's tooted his little horn, and you an' me has turned up missing," remarked Hootchinoo Bill.

His remark was casual, as though there was nothing unusual about the occurrence. Kink

Mitchell's reply was just as casual as though he, too, were unaware of any strange perturbation of spirit.

"Looks as they was all Baptists, then, and took the boats to go by water," was his contribution.

"My ol' dad was a Baptist," Hootchinoo Bill supplemented. "An' he always did hold it was forty thousand miles nearer that way."

This was the end of their levity. They ran the canoe in and climbed the high earth bank. A feeling of awe descended upon them as they walked the deserted streets. The sunlight streamed placidly over the town. A gentle wind tapped the halyards against the flagpole before the closed doors of the Caledonia Dance Hall. Mosquitoes buzzed, robins sang, and moose birds tripped hungrily among the cabins; but there was no human life nor sign of human life.

"I'm just dyin' for a drink," Hootchinoo Bill said, and unconsciously his voice sank to a hoarse whisper.

His partner nodded his head, loth to hear

his own voice break the stillness. They trudged on in uneasy silence till surprised by an open door. Above this door, and stretching the width of the building, a rude sign announced the same as the "Monte Carlo." But beside the door, hat over eyes, chair tilted back, a man sat sunning himself. He was an old man. Beard and hair were long and white and patriarchal.

"If it ain't ol' Jim Cummings, turned up like us, too late for Resurrection!" said Kink Mitchell.

"Most like he didn't hear Gabriel tootin'," was Hootchinoo Bill's suggestion.

"Hello, Jim! Wake up!" he shouted.

The old man unlimbered lamely, blinking his eyes and murmuring automatically: "What'll ye have, gents? What'll ye have?"

They followed him inside and ranged up against the long bar where of yore a half-dozen nimble barkeepers found little time to loaf. The great room, ordinarily aroar with life, was still and gloomy as a tomb. There was no rattling of chips, no whirring of ivory balls.

Roulette and faro tables were like gravestones
under their canvas covers.   No women's voices
drifted merrily from the dance room behind.
Ol' Jim Cummings wiped a glass with palsied
hands, and Kink Mitchell scrawled his initials
on the dust-covered bar.

"Where's the girls?" Hootchinoo Bill
shouted, with affected geniality.

"Gone," was the ancient barkeeper's reply,
in a voice thin and aged as himself, and as
unsteady as his hand.

"Where's Bidwell and Barlow?"

"Gone."

"And Sweetwater Charley?"

"Gone."

"And his sister?"

"Gone, too."

"Your daughter Sally, then, and her little
kid?"

"Gone, all gone." The old man shook his
head sadly, rummaging in an absent way among
the dusty bottles.

"Great Sardanapolis! Where?" Kink
Mitchell exploded, unable longer to restrain

himself. "You don't say you've had the plague?"

"Why, ain't you heerd?" The old man chuckled quietly. "They-all's gone to Dawson."

"What-like is that?" Bill demanded. "A creek? or a bar? or a place?"

"Ain't never heered of Dawson, eh?" The old man chuckled exasperatingly. "Why, Dawson's a town, a city, bigger'n Forty Mile. Yes, sir, bigger'n Forty Mile."

"I've ben in this land seven year," Bill announced emphatically, "an' I make free to say I never heard tell of the burg before. Hold on! Let's have some more of that whiskey. Your information's flabbergasted me, that it has. Now just whereabouts is this Dawson-place you was a-mentionin'?"

"On the big flat jest below the mouth of Klondike," ol' Jim answered. "But where has you-all ben this summer?"

"Never you mind where we-all's ben," was Kink Mitchell's testy reply. "We-all's ben where the skeeters is that thick you've got to throw a stick into the air so as to see the sun and tell the time of day. Ain't I right, Bill?"

"Right you are," said Bill. "But speakin' of this Dawson-place, how like did it happen to be, Jim?"

"Ounce to the pan on a creek called Bonanza, an' they ain't got to bed-rock yet."

"Who struck it?"

"Carmack."

At mention of the discoverer's name the partners stared at each other disgustedly. Then they winked with great solemnity.

"Siwash George," sniffed Hootchinoo Bill.

"That squaw-man," sneered Kink Mitchell.

"I wouldn't put on my moccasins to stampede after anything he'd ever find," said Bill.

"Same here," announced his partner. "A cuss that's too plumb lazy to fish his own salmon. That's why he took up with the Indians. S'pose that black brother-in-law of his, — lemme see, Skookum Jim, eh? — s'pose he's in on it?"

The old barkeeper nodded. "Sure, an'

what's more, all Forty Mile, exceptin' me an'
a few cripples."

"And drunks," added Kink Mitchell.

"No-sir-ee!" the old man shouted emphatically.

"I bet you the drinks Honkins ain't in on
it!" Hootchinoo Bill cried with certitude.

Ol' Jim's face lighted up. "I takes you,
Bill, an' you loses."

"However did that ol' soak budge out of
Forty Mile?" Mitchell demanded.

"They ties him down an' throws him in the
bottom of a polin'-boat," ol' Jim explained.
"Come right in here, they did, an' takes him
out of that there chair there in the corner, an'
three more drunks they finds under the piany.
I tell you-alls the whole camp hits up the
Yukon for Dawson jes' like Sam Scratch was
after them, — wimmen, children, babes in arms,
the whole shebang. Bidwell comes to me an'
sez, sez he, 'Jim, I wants you to keep tab on
the Monte Carlo. I'm goin'.'

"'Where's Barlow?' sez I. 'Gone,' sez
he, 'an' I'm a-followin' with a load of whis-

key.' An' with that, never waitin' for me to decline, he makes a run for his boat an' away he goes, polin' up river like mad. So here I be, an' these is the first drinks I've passed out in three days."

The partners looked at each other.

"Gosh darn my buttons!" said Hootchinoo Bill. "Seems like you and me, Kink, is the kind of folks always caught out with forks when it rains soup."

"Wouldn't it take the saleratus out your dough, now?" said Kink Mitchell. "A stampede of tin horns, drunks, an' loafers."

"An' squaw-men," added Bill. "Not a genooine miner in the whole caboodle."

"Genooine miners like you an' me, Kink," he went on academically, "is all out an' sweatin' hard over Birch Creek way. Not a genooine miner in this whole crazy Dawson outfit, and I say right here, not a step do I budge for any Carmack strike. I've got to see the color of the dust first."

"Same here," Mitchell agreed. "Let's have another drink."

Having wet this resolution, they beached the canoe, transferred its contents to their cabin, and cooked dinner. But as the afternoon wore along they grew restive. They were men used to the silence of the great wilderness, but this gravelike silence of a town worried them. They caught themselves listening for familiar sounds — "waitin' for something to make a noise which ain't goin' to make a noise," as Bill put it. They strolled through the deserted streets to the Monte Carlo for more drinks, and wandered along the river bank to the steamer landing, where only water gurgled as the eddy filled and emptied, and an occasional salmon leapt flashing into the sun.

They sat down in the shade in front of the store and talked with the consumptive storekeeper, whose liability to hemorrhage accounted for his presence. Bill and Kink told him how they intended loafing in their cabin and resting up after the hard summer's work. They told him, with a certain insistence, that was half appeal for belief, half challenge for contradic-

tion, how much they were going to enjoy their
idleness.   But the storekeeper was uninterested.
He switched the conversation back to the
strike on Klondike, and they could not keep
him away from it.   He could think of nothing else, talk of nothing else, till Hootchinoo
Bill rose up in anger and disgust.

"Gosh darn Dawson, say I!" he cried.

"Same here," said Kink Mitchell, with a
brightening face.   "One'd think something was
doin' up there, 'stead of bein' a mere stampede
of greenhorns an' tinhorns."

But a boat came into view from down-
stream.   It was long and slim.   It hugged
the bank closely, and its three occupants,
standing upright, propelled it against the stiff
current by means of long poles.

"Circle City outfit," said the storekeeper.
"I was lookin' for 'em along by afternoon.
Forty Mile had the start of them by a hundred
and seventy miles.   But gee! they ain't losin'
any time!"

"We'll just sit here quietlike and watch 'em
string by," Bill said complacently.

As he spoke, another boat appeared in sight, followed after a brief interval by two others. By this time the first boat was abreast of the men on the bank. Its occupants did not cease poling while greetings were exchanged, and, though its progress was slow, a half hour saw it out of sight up river.

Still they came from below, boat after boat, in endless procession. The uneasiness of Bill and Kink increased. They stole speculative, tentative glances at each other, and when their eyes met, looked away in embarrassment. Finally, however, their eyes met and neither looked away.

Kink opened his mouth to speak, but words failed him and his mouth remained open while he continued to gaze at his partner.

"Just what I was thinkin', Kink," said Bill.

They grinned sheepishly at each other, and by tacit consent started to walk away. Their pace quickened, and by the time they arrived at their cabin they were on the run.

"Can't lose no time with all that multitude a-rushin' by," Kink spluttered, as he jabbed the sour-dough can into the beanpot with one hand and with the other gathered in the frying-pan and coffee-pot.

"Should say not," gasped Bill, his head and shoulders buried in a clothes-sack wherein were stored winter socks and underwear. "I say, Kink, don't forget the saleratus on the corner shelf back of the stove."

Half an hour later they were launching the canoe and loading up, while the storekeeper made jocular remarks about poor, weak mortals and the contagiousness of "stampedin' fever." But when Bill and Kink thrust their long poles to bottom and started the canoe against the current, he called after them: —

"Well, so long and good luck! And don't forget to blaze a stake or two for me!"

They nodded their heads vigorously and felt sorry for the poor wretch who remained perforce behind.

*   *   *   *   *   *

Kink and Bill were sweating hard. According to the revised Northland Scripture, the stampede is to the swift, the blazing of stakes

to the strong, and the Crown, in royalties,
gathers to itself the fulness thereof. Kink
and Bill were both swift and strong. They
took the soggy trail at a long, swinging gait
that broke the hearts of a couple of tenderfeet
who tried to keep up with them. Behind,
strung out between them and Dawson (where
the boats were discarded and land travel
began), was the vanguard of the Circle City
outfit. In the race from Forty Mile the
partners had passed every boat, winning from
the leading boat by a length in the Dawson
eddy and leaving its occupants sadly behind
the moment their feet struck the trail.

"Huh! couldn't see us for smoke,"
Hootchinoo Bill chuckled, flirting the stinging sweat from his brow and glancing swiftly
back along the way they had come.

Three men emerged from where the trail
broke through the trees. Two followed close
at their heels, and then a man and a woman
shot into view.

"Come on, you Kink! Hit her up! Hit
her up!"

Bill quickened his pace.   Mitchell glanced
back in more leisurely fashion.

"I declare if they ain't lopin'!"

"And here's one that's loped himself out,"
said Bill, pointing to the side of the trail.

A man was lying on his back, panting, in
the culminating stages of violent exhaustion.
His face was ghastly, his eyes blood-shot and
glazed, for all the world like a dying man.

"*Chechaquo!*" Kink Mitchell grunted, and
it was the grunt of the old "sour dough"
for the greenhorn, for the man who outfitted
with "self-risin'" flour and used baking powder in his biscuits.

The partners, true to the old-timer custom, had intended to stake down-stream from
the strike, but when they saw claim 81 Below
blazed on a tree, — which meant fully eight
miles below Discovery, — they changed their
minds.   The eight miles were covered in less
than two hours.   It was a killing pace, over
so rough trail, and they passed scores of
exhausted men that had fallen by the way-
side.

At Discovery little was to be learned of the upper creek. Carmack's Indian brother-in-law, Skookum Jim, had a hazy notion that the creek was staked as high as the 30's; but when Kink and Bill looked at the corner-stakes of 79 Above, they threw their stamped-ing packs off their backs and sat down to smoke. All their effort had been vain. Bonanza was staked from mouth to source, — "out of sight and across the next divide," Bill complained that night as they fried their bacon and boiled their coffee over Carmack's fire at Discovery.

"Try that pup," Carmack suggested next morning.

"That pup" was a broad creek that flowed into Bonanza at 7 Above. The partners received his advice with the magnificent contempt of the sour dough for a squaw-man, and, instead, spent the day on Adam's Creek, another and more likely-looking tributary of Bonanza. But it was the old story over again — staked to the sky-line.

For three days Carmack repeated his advice,

and for three days they received it contemptu-
ously.   But on the fourth day, there being
nowhere else to go, they went up "that pup."
They knew that it was practically unstaked,
but they had no intention of staking.   The
trip was made more for the purpose of giving
vent to their ill-humor than for anything else.
They had become quite cynical, sceptical.
They jeered and scoffed at everything, and
insulted every *chechaquo* they met along the
way.

At No. 23 the stakes ceased.   The remainder of the creek was open to location.

"Moose pasture!" sneered Kink Mitchell.

But Bill gravely paced off five hundred feet
up the creek and blazed the corner-stakes.
He had picked up the bottom of a candle-
box, and on the smooth side he wrote the
notice for his centre-stake: —

THIS MOOSE PASTURE IS RESERVED FOR THE
SWEDES AND CHECHAQUOS
— BILL RADER.

Kink read it over with approval, saying: —

"As them's my sentiments, I reckon I might as well subscribe."

So the name of Charles Mitchell was added to the notice; and many an old sour dough's face relaxed that day at sight of the handiwork of a kindred spirit.

"How's the pup?" Carmack inquired when they strolled back into camp.

"To hell with pups!" was Hootchinoo Bill's reply. "Me and Kink's goin' a-lookin' for Too Much Gold when we get rested up."

Too Much Gold was the fabled creek of which all sour doughs dreamed, whereof it was said the gold was so thick that, in order to wash it, gravel must first be shovelled into the sluice-boxes. But the several days' rest, preliminary to the quest for Too Much Gold, brought a slight change in their plan, inasmuch as it brought one Ans Handerson, a Swede.

Ans Handerson had been working for wages all summer at Miller Creek, over on the Sixty Mile, and, the summer done, had strayed up

Bonanza like many another waif helplessly
adrift on the gold tides that swept willy-nilly
across the land. He was tall and lanky. His
arms were long, like prehistoric man's, and
his hands were like soup-plates, twisted and
gnarled, and big-knuckled from toil. He was
slow of utterance and movement, and his eyes,
pale blue as his hair was pale yellow, seemed
filled with an immortal dreaming, the stuff of
which no man knew, and himself least of all.
Perhaps this appearance of immortal dreaming
was due to a supreme and vacuous innocence.
At any rate, this was the valuation men of
ordinary clay put upon him, and there was
nothing extraordinary about the composition
of Hootchinoo Bill and Kink Mitchell.

The partners had spent a day of visiting and
gossip, and in the evening met in the tempo-
rary quarters of the Monte Carlo — a large
tent where stampeders rested their weary bones
and bad whiskey sold at a dollar a drink.
Since the only money in circulation was dust,
and since the house took the " down-weight "
on the scales, a drink cost something more

than a dollar.   Bill and Kink were not drinking, principally for the reason that their one
and common sack was not strong enough to
stand many excursions to the scales.

"Say, Bill, I've got a *chechaquo* on the
string for a sack of flour," Mitchell announced
jubilantly.

Bill looked interested and pleased.   Grub
was scarce, and they were not overplentifully
supplied for the quest after Too Much Gold.

"Flour's worth a dollar a pound," he
answered.   "How like do you calculate to
get your finger on it?"

"Trade'm a half-interest in that claim of
our'n," Kink answered.

"What claim?" Bill was surprised.   Then
he remembered the reservation he had staked
off for the Swedes, and said, "Oh!"

"I wouldn't be so clost about it, though,"
he added.   "Give'm the whole thing while
you're about it, in a right free-handed way."

Bill shook his head.   "If I did, he'd get
clean scairt and prance off.   I'm lettin' on as
how the ground is believed to be valuable, an'

that we're lettin' go half just because we're monstrous short on grub. After the dicker we can make him a present of the whole shebang."

"If somebody ain't disregarded our notice," Bill objected, though he was plainly pleased at the prospect of exchanging the claim for a sack of flour.

"She ain't jumped," Kink assured him. "It's No. 24, and it stands. The *chechaquos* took it serious, and they begun stakin' where you left off. Staked clean over the divide, too. I was gassin' with one of them which has just got in with cramps in his legs."

It was then, and for the first time, that they heard the slow and groping utterance of Ans Handerson.

"Ay like the looks," he was saying to the barkeeper. "Ay tank Ay gat a claim."

The partners winked at each other, and a few minutes later a surprised and grateful Swede was drinking bad whiskey with two hard-hearted strangers. But he was as hard headed as they were hard hearted. The sack

made frequent journeys to the scales, followed
solicitously each time by Kink Mitchell's
eyes, and still Ans Handerson did not loosen
up. In his pale blue eyes, as in summer seas,
immortal dreams swam up and burned, but
the swimming and the burning were due to the
tales of gold and prospect pans he heard,
rather than to the whiskey he slid so easily
down his throat.

The partners were in despair, though they
appeared boisterous and jovial of speech and
action.

"Don't mind me, my friend," Hootchinoo
Bill hiccoughed, his hand upon Ans Han-
derson's shoulder. "Have another drink.
We're just celebratin' Kink's birthday here.
This is my pardner Kink, Kink Mitchell.
An' what might your name be?"

This learned, his hand descended resound-
ingly on Kink's back, and Kink simulated
clumsy self-consciousness in that he was for
the time being the centre of the rejoicing,
while Ans Handerson looked pleased and
asked them to have a drink with him. It was

the first and last time he treated, until the play changed and his canny soul was roused to unwonted prodigality. But he paid for the liquor from a fairly healthy-looking sack. " Not less'n eight hundred in it," calculated the lynx-eyed Kink; and on the strength of it he took the first opportunity of a privy conversation with Bidwell, proprietor of the bad whiskey and the tent.

" Here's my sack, Bidwell," Kink said, with the intimacy and surety of one old-timer to another. " Just weigh fifty dollars into it for a day or so more or less, and we'll be yours truly, Bill an' me."

Thereafter the journeys of the sack to the scales were more frequent, and the celebration of Kink's natal day waxed hilarious. He even essayed to sing the old-timer's classic, " The Juice of the Forbidden Fruit," but broke down and drowned his embarrassment in another round of drinks. Even Bidwell honored him with a round or two on the house; and he and Bill were decently drunk by the time Ans Handerson's eyelids began to droop and his tongue gave promise of loosening.

Bill grew affectionate, then confidential. He told his troubles and hard luck to the bar-keeper and the world in general, and to Ans Handerson in particular. He required no histrionic powers to act the part. The bad whiskey attended to that. He worked himself into a great sorrow for himself and Bill, and his tears were sincere when he told how he and his partner were thinking of selling a half-interest in good ground just because they were short of grub. Even Kink listened and believed.

Ans Handerson's eyes were shining unholily as he asked, "How much you tank you take?"

Bill and Kink did not hear him, and he was compelled to repeat his query. They appeared reluctant. He grew keener. And he swayed back and forward, holding on to the bar and listening with all his ears while they conferred together on one side, and wrangled as to whether they should or not, and disagreed in stage whispers over the price they should set.

"Two hundred and — hic! — fifty," Bill finally announced, "but we reckon as we won't sell."

"Which is monstrous wise if I might chip in my little say," seconded Bidwell.

"Yes, indeedy," added Kink. "We ain't in no charity business a-disgorgin' free an' generous to Swedes an' white men."

"Ay tank we haf another drink," hiccoughed Ans Handerson, craftily changing the subject against a more propitious time.

And thereafter, to bring about that propitious time, his own sack began to see-saw between his hip pocket and the scales. Bill and Kink were coy, but they finally yielded to his blandishments. Whereupon he grew shy and drew Bidwell to one side. He staggered exceedingly, and held on to Bidwell for support as he asked: —

"They ban all right, them men, you tank so?"

"Sure," Bidwell answered heartily. "Known

'em for years. Old sour doughs. When they sell a claim, they sell a claim. They ain't no air-dealers."

"Ay tank Ay buy," Ans Handerson announced, tottering back to the two men.

But by now he was dreaming deeply, and he proclaimed he would have the whole claim or nothing. This was the cause of great pain to Hootchinoo Bill. He orated grandly against the "hawgishness" of *chechaquos* and Swedes, albeit he dozed between periods, his voice dying away to a gurgle, and his head sinking forward on his breast. But whenever roused by a nudge from Kink or Bidwell, he never failed to explode another volley of abuse and insult.

Ans Handerson was calm under it all. Each insult added to the value of the claim. Such unamiable reluctance to sell advertised but one thing to him, and he was aware of a great relief when Hootchinoo Bill sank snoring to the floor, and he was free to turn his attention to his less intractable partner.

Kink Mitchell was persuadable, though a poor mathematician. He wept dolefully, but was willing to sell a half-interest for two hundred and fifty dollars or the whole claim for seven hundred and fifty. Ans Handerson and Bidwell labored to clear away his erroneous ideas concerning fractions, but their labor was vain. He spilled tears and regrets all over the bar and on their shoulders, which tears, however, did not wash away his opinion, that if one half was worth two hundred and fifty, two halves were worth three times as much.

In the end, — and even Bidwell retained no more than hazy recollections of how the night terminated, — a bill of sale was drawn up, wherein Bill Rader and Charles Mitchell yielded up all right and title to the claim known as **24 Eldorado**, the same being the name the creek had received from some optimistic *chechaquo*.

When Kink had signed, it took the united efforts of the three to arouse Bill. Pen in hand, he swayed long over the document; and, each time he rocked back and forth, in

Ans Handerson's eyes flashed and faded a wondrous golden vision. When the precious signature was at last appended and the dust paid over, he breathed a great sigh, and sank to sleep under a table, where he dreamed immortally until morning.

But the day was chill and gray. He felt bad. His first act, unconscious and automatic, was to feel for his sack. Its lightness startled him. Then, slowly, memories of the night thronged into his brain. Rough voices disturbed him. He opened his eyes and peered out from under the table. A couple of early risers, or, rather, men who had been out on trail all night, were vociferating their opinions concerning the utter and loathsome worthlessness of Eldorado Creek. He grew frightened, felt in his pocket, and found the deed to 24 Eldorado.

Ten minutes later Hootchinoo Bill and Kink Mitchell were roused from their blankets by a wild-eyed Swede that strove to force upon them an ink-scrawled and very blotty piece of paper.

"Ay tank Ay take my money back," he gibbered. "Ay tank Ay take my money back."

Tears were in his eyes and throat. They ran down his cheeks as he knelt before them and pleaded and implored. But Bill and Kink did not laugh. They might have been harder hearted.

"First time I ever hear a man squeal over a minin' deal," Bill said. "An' I make free to say 'tis too onusual for me to savvy."

"Same here," Kink Mitchell remarked. "Minin' deals is like horse-tradin'."

They were honest in their wonderment. They could not conceive of themselves raising a wail over a business transaction, so they could not understand it in another man.

"The poor, ornery *chechaquo*," murmured Hootchinoo Bill, as they watched the sorrowing Swede disappear up the trail.

"But this ain't Too Much Gold," Kink Mitchell said cheerfully.

And ere the day was out they purchased flour and bacon at exorbitant prices with Ans

Handerson's dust and crossed over the divide in the direction of the creeks that lie between Klondike and Indian River.

Three months later they came back over the divide in the midst of a snow storm and dropped down the trail to 24 Eldorado. It merely chanced that the trail led them that way. They were not looking for the claim. Nor could they see much through the driving white till they set foot upon the claim itself. And then the air lightened, and they beheld a dump, capped by a windlass that a man was turning. They saw him draw a bucket of gravel from the hole and tilt it on the edge of the dump. Likewise they saw another man, strangely familiar, filling a pan with the fresh gravel. His hands were large; his hair was pale yellow. But before they reached him, he turned with the pan and fled toward a cabin. He wore no hat, and the snow falling down his neck accounted for his haste. Bill and Kink ran after him, and came upon him in the cabin, kneeling by the stove and washing the pan of gravel in a tub of water.

He was too deeply engaged to notice more than that somebody had entered the cabin. They stood at his shoulder and looked on. He imparted to the pan a deft circular motion, pausing once or twice to rake out the larger particles of gravel with his fingers. The water was muddy, and, with the pan buried in it, they could see nothing of its contents. Suddenly he lifted the pan clear and sent the water out of it with a flirt. A mass of yellow, like butter in a churn, showed across the bottom.

Hootchinoo Bill swallowed. Never in his life had he dreamed of so rich a test-pan.

" Kind of thick, my friend," he said huskily. " How much might you reckon that-all to be ? "

Ans Handerson did not look up as he replied, " Ay tank fafty ounces."

" You must be scrumptious rich, then, eh ? "

Still Ans Handerson kept his head down, absorbed in putting in the fine touches which wash out the last particles of dross, though he answered, "Ay tank Ay ban wort' five hundred t'ousand dollar."

"Gosh!" said Hootchinoo Bill, and he said it reverently.

"Yes, Bill, gosh!" said Kink Mitchell; and they went out softly and closed the door.

THE ONE THOUSAND DOZEN

THE ONE THOUSAND DOZEN

D AVID RASMUNSEN was a hustler, and, like many a greater man, a man of the one idea. Wherefore, when the clarion call of the North rang on his ear, he conceived an adventure in eggs and bent all his energy to its achievement. He figured briefly and to the point, and the adventure became iridescent-hued, splendid. That eggs would sell at Dawson for five dollars a dozen was a safe working premise. Whence it was incontrovertible that one thousand dozen would bring, in the Golden Metropolis, five thousand dollars.

On the other hand, expense was to be considered, and he considered it well, for he was a careful man, keenly practical, with a hard head and a heart that imagination never warmed. At fifteen cents a dozen, the initial cost of his

thousand dozen would be one hundred and
fifty dollars, a mere bagatelle in face of the
enormous profit.   And suppose, just suppose,
to be wildly extravagant for once, that trans-
portation for himself and eggs should run up
eight hundred and fifty more; he would still
have four thousand clear cash and clean when
the last egg was disposed of and the last dust
had rippled into his sack.

   " You see, Alma," — he figured it over with
his wife, the cosy dining room submerged in a
sea of maps, government surveys, guidebooks,
and Alaskan itineraries, — " you see, expenses
don't really begin till you make Dyea — fifty
dollars'll cover it with a first-class passage
thrown in.   Now from Dyea to Lake Linderman, Indian packers take your goods over for
twelve cents a pound, twelve dollars a hundred,
or one hundred and twenty dollars a thousand.
Say I have fifteen hundred pounds, it'll cost
one hundred and eighty dollars — call it two
hundred and be safe.   I am creditably informed
by a Klondiker just come out that I can buy a
boat for three hundred.   But the same man

says I'm sure to get a couple of passengers for one hundred and fifty each, which will give me the boat for nothing, and, further, they can help me manage it. And . . . that's all; I put my eggs ashore from the boat at Dawson. Now let me see how much is that?"

"Fifty dollars from San Francisco to Dyea, two hundred from Dyea to Linderman, passengers pay for the boat — two hundred and fifty all told," she summed up swiftly.

"And a hundred for my clothes and personal outfit," he went on happily; "that leaves a margin of five hundred for emergencies. And what possible emergencies can arise?"

Alma shrugged her shoulders and elevated her brows. If that vast Northland was capable of swallowing up a man and a thousand dozen eggs, surely there was room and to spare for whatever else he might happen to possess. So she thought, but she said nothing. She knew David Rasmunsen too well to say anything.

"Doubling the time because of chance delays, I should make the trip in two months. Think of it, Alma! Four thousand in two months! Beats the paltry hundred a month I'm getting now. Why, we'll build further out where we'll have more space, gas in every room, and a view, and the rent of the cottage'll pay taxes, insurance, and water, and leave something over. And then there's always the chance of my striking it and coming out a millionnaire. Now tell me, Alma, don't you think I'm very moderate?"

And Alma could hardly think otherwise. Besides, had not her own cousin, — though a remote and distant one to be sure, the black sheep, the harum-scarum, the ne'er-do-well, — had not he come down out of that weird North country with a hundred thousand in yellow dust, to say nothing of a half-ownership in the hole from which it came?

David Rasmunsen's grocer was surprised when he found him weighing eggs in the scales at the end of the counter, and Rasmunsen himself was more surprised when he found that a dozen eggs weighed a pound and a half — fifteen hundred pounds for his thou-

sand dozen! There would be no weight left
for his clothes, blankets, and cooking utensils,
to say nothing of the grub he must necessarily
consume by the way. His calculations were
all thrown out, and he was just proceeding to
recast them when he hit upon the idea of
weighing small eggs. "For whether they be
large or small, a dozen eggs is a dozen eggs,"
he observed sagely to himself; and a dozen
small ones he found to weigh but a pound
and a quarter. Thereat the city of San Francisco was overrun by anxious-eyed emissaries,
and commission houses and dairy associations
were startled by a sudden demand for eggs
running not more than twenty ounces to the
dozen.

Rasmunsen mortgaged the little cottage for a
thousand dollars, arranged for his wife to make
a prolonged stay among her own people, threw
up his job, and started North. To keep within
his schedule he compromised on a second-class
passage, which, because of the rush, was worse
than steerage; and in the late summer, a pale
and wabbly man, he disembarked with his eggs

on the Dyea beach. But it did not take him long to recover his land legs and appetite. His first interview with the Chilkoot packers straightened him up and stiffened his backbone. Forty cents a pound they demanded for the twenty-eight-mile portage, and while he caught his breath and swallowed, the price went up to forty-three. Fifteen husky Indians put the straps on his packs at forty-five, but took them off at an offer of forty-seven from a Skaguay Crœsus in dirty shirt and ragged overalls who had lost his horses on the White Pass Trail and was now making a last desperate drive at the country by way of Chilkoot.

But Rasmunsen was clean grit, and at fifty cents found takers, who, two days later, set his eggs down intact at Linderman. But fifty cents a pound is a thousand dollars a ton, and his fifteen hundred pounds had exhausted his emergency fund and left him stranded at the Tantalus point where each day he saw the fresh-whipsawed boats departing for Dawson. Further, a great anxiety brooded over the camp where the boats were built. Men worked

frantically, early and late, at the height of their
endurance, calking, nailing, and pitching in a
frenzy of haste for which adequate explanation
was not far to seek. Each day the snow-line
crept farther down the bleak, rock-shouldered
peaks, and gale followed gale, with sleet and
slush and snow, and in the eddies and quiet
places young ice formed and thickened through
the fleeting hours. And each morn, toil-stif-
fened men turned wan faces across the lake to
see if the freeze-up had come. For the freeze-
up heralded the death of their hope — the hope
that they would be floating down the swift
river ere navigation closed on the chain of
lakes.

To harrow Rasmunsen's soul further, he
discovered three competitors in the egg business. It was true that one, a little German,
had gone broke and was himself forlornly
back-tripping the last pack of the portage; but
the other two had boats nearly completed and
were daily supplicating the god of merchants
and traders to stay the iron hand of winter for
just another day. But the iron hand closed

down over the land. Men were being frozen in the blizzard, which swept Chilkoot, and Rasmunsen frosted his toes ere he was aware. He found a chance to go passenger with his freight in a boat just shoving off through the rubble, but two hundred, hard cash, was required, and he had no money.

"Ay tank you yust wait one leedle w'ile," said the Swedish boat-builder, who had struck his Klondike right there and was wise enough to know it — "one leedle w'ile und I make you a tam fine skiff boat, sure Pete."

With this unpledged word to go on, Rasmunsen hit the back trail to Crater Lake, where he fell in with two press correspondents whose tangled baggage was strewn from Stone House, over across the Pass, and as .far as Happy Camp.

"Yes," he said with consequence. "I've a thousand dozen eggs at Linderman, and my boat's just about got the last seam calked. Consider myself in luck to get it. Boats are at a premium, you know, and none to be had."

Whereupon and almost with bodily violence the correspondents clamored to go with him, fluttered greenbacks before his eyes, and spilled yellow twenties from hand to hand. He could not hear of it, but they overpersuaded him, and he reluctantly consented to take them at three hundred apiece. Also they pressed upon him the passage money in advance. And while they wrote to their respective journals concerning the good Samaritan with the thousand dozen eggs, the good Samaritan was hurrying back to the Swede at Linderman.

"Here, you! Gimme that boat!" was his salutation, his hand jingling the correspondents' gold pieces and his eyes hungrily bent upon the finished craft.

The Swede regarded him stolidly and shook his head.

"How much is the other fellow paying? Three hundred? Well, here's four. Take it."

He tried to press it upon him, but the man backed away.

"Ay tank not. Ay say him get der skiff boat. You yust wait —"

"Here's six hundred. Last call. Take it or leave it. Tell'm it's a mistake."

The Swede wavered. "Ay tank yes," he finally said, and the last Rasmunsen saw of him his vocabulary was going to wreck in a vain effort to explain the mistake to the other fellows.

The German slipped and broke his ankle on the steep hogback above Deep Lake, sold out his stock for a dollar a dozen, and with the proceeds hired Indian packers to carry him back to Dyea. But on the morning Rasmunsen shoved off with his correspondents, his two rivals followed suit.

"How many you got?" one of them, a lean little New Englander, called out.

"One thousand dozen," Rasmunsen answered proudly.

"Huh! I'll go you even stakes I beat you in with my eight hundred."

The correspondents offered to lend him the money; but Rasmunsen declined, and the

Yankee closed with the remaining rival, a brawny son of the sea and sailor of ships and things, who promised to show them all a wrinkle or two when it came to cracking on. And crack on he did, with a large tarpaulin squaresail which pressed the bow half under at every jump. He was the first to run out of Linderman, but, disdaining the portage, piled his loaded boat on the rocks in the boiling rapids. Rasmunsen and the Yankee, who likewise had two passengers, portaged across on their backs and then lined their empty boats down through the bad water to Bennett.

Bennett was a twenty-five-mile lake, narrow and deep, a funnel between the mountains through which storms ever romped. Rasmunsen camped on the sand-pit at its head, where were many men and boats bound north in the teeth of the Arctic winter. He awoke in the morning to find a piping gale from the south, which caught the chill from the whited peaks and glacial valleys and blew as cold as north wind ever blew. But it was fair, and he also found the Yankee staggering past the first bold headland with all sail set. Boat after boat was getting under way, and the correspondents fell to with enthusiasm.

"We'll catch him before Cariboo Crossing," they assured Rasmunsen, as they ran up the sail and the *Alma* took the first icy spray over her bow.

Now Rasmunsen all his life had been prone to cowardice on water, but he clung to the kicking steering-oar with set face and determined jaw. His thousand dozen were there in the boat before his eyes, safely secured beneath the correspondents' baggage, and somehow, before his eyes, were the little cottage and the mortgage for a thousand dollars.

It was bitter cold. Now and again he hauled in the steering-sweep and put out a fresh one while his passengers chopped the ice from the blade. Wherever the spray struck, it turned instantly to frost, and the dipping boom of the spritsail was quickly fringed with icicles. The *Alma* strained and

hammered through the big seas till the seams
and butts began to spread, but in lieu of bailing the correspondents chopped ice and flung
it overboard. There was no let-up. The
mad race with winter was on, and the boats
tore along in a desperate string.

"W-w-we can't stop to save our souls!"
one of the correspondents chattered, from cold,
not fright.

"That's right! Keep her down the middle,
old man!" the other encouraged.

Rasmunsen replied with an idiotic grin.
The iron-bound shores were in a lather of
foam, and even down the middle the only
hope was to keep running away from the big
seas. To lower sail was to be overtaken and
swamped. Time and again they passed boats
pounding among the rocks, and once they saw
one on the edge of the breakers about to
strike. A little craft behind them, with two
men, jibed over and turned bottom up.

"W-w-watch out, old man!" cried he of
the chattering teeth.

Rasmunsen grinned and tightened his aching

grip on the sweep. Scores of times had the send of the sea caught the big square stern of the *Alma* and thrown her off from dead before it till the after leach of the spritsail fluttered hollowly, and each time, and only with all his strength, had he forced her back. His grin by then had become fixed, and it disturbed the correspondents to look at him.

They roared down past an isolated rock a hundred yards from shore. From its wave-drenched top a man shrieked wildly, for the instant cutting the storm with his voice. But the next instant the *Alma* was by, and the rock growing a black speck in the troubled froth.

"That settles the Yankee! Where's the sailor?" shouted one of his passengers.

Rasmunsen shot a glance over his shoulder at a black squaresail. He had seen it leap up out of the gray to windward, and for an hour, off and on, had been watching it grow. The sailor had evidently repaired damages and was making up for lost time.

"Look at him come!"

Both passengers stopped chopping ice to

watch. Twenty miles of Bennett were behind them — room and to spare for the sea to toss up its mountains toward the sky. Sinking and soaring like a storm god, the sailor drove by them. The huge sail seemed to grip the boat from the crests of the waves, to tear it bodily out of the water, and fling it crashing and smothering down into the yawning troughs.

" The sea'll never catch him ! "

" But he'll r-r-run her nose under ! "

Even as they spoke, the black tarpaulin swooped from sight behind a big comber. The next wave rolled over the spot, and the next, but the boat did not reappear. The *Alma* rushed by the place. A little riffraff of oars and boxes was seen. An arm thrust up and a shaggy head broke surface a score of yards away.

For a time there was silence. As the end of the lake came in sight, the waves began to leap aboard with such steady recurrence that the correspondents no longer chopped ice but flung the water out with buckets. Even this would not do, and, after a shouted conference with Rasmunsen, they attacked the baggage. Flour, bacon, beans, blankets, cooking stove, ropes, odds and ends, everything they could get hands on, flew overboard. The boat acknowledged it at once, taking less water and rising more buoyantly.

"That'll do!" Rasmunsen called sternly, as they applied themselves to the top layer of eggs.

"The h-hell it will!" answered the shivering one, savagely. With the exception of their notes, films, and cameras, they had sacrificed their outfit. He bent over, laid hold of an egg-box, and began to worry it out from under the lashing.

"Drop it! Drop it, I say!"

Rasmunsen had managed to draw his revolver, and with the crook of his arm over the sweep head was taking aim. The correspondent stood up on the thwart, balancing back and forth, his face twisted with menace and speechless anger.

"My God!"

So cried his brother correspondent, hurling

himself, face downward, into the bottom of
the boat. The *Alma*, under the divided attention of Rasmunsen, had been caught by a great
mass of water and whirled around. The after
leach hollowed, the sail emptied and jibed, and
the boom, sweeping with terrific force across
the boat, carried the angry correspondent
overboard with a broken back. Mast and
sail had gone over the side as well. A
drenching sea followed, as the boat lost
headway, and Rasmunsen sprang to the
bailing bucket.

Several boats hurtled past them in the next
half-hour, — small boats, boats of their own
size, boats afraid, unable to do aught but run
madly on. Then a ten-ton barge, at imminent
risk of destruction, lowered sail to windward
and lumbered down upon them.

" Keep off! Keep off!" Rasmunsen
screamed.

But his low gunwale ground against the
heavy craft, and the remaining correspondent
clambered aboard. Rasmunsen was over the
eggs like a cat and in the bow of the *Alma*,

striving with numb fingers to bend the hauling-lines together.

"Come on!" a red-whiskered man yelled at him.

"I've a thousand dozen eggs here," he shouted back. "Gimme a tow! I'll pay you!"

"Come on!" they howled in chorus.

A big whitecap broke just beyond, washing over the barge and leaving the *Alma* half swamped. The men cast off, cursing him as they ran up their sail. Rasmunsen cursed back and fell to bailing. The mast and sail, like a sea anchor, still fast by the halyards, held the boat head on to wind and sea and gave him a chance to fight the water out.

Three hours later, numbed, exhausted, blathering like a lunatic, but still bailing, he went ashore on an ice-strewn beach near Cariboo Crossing. Two men, a government courier and a half-breed voyageur, dragged him out of the surf, saved his cargo, and beached the *Alma*. They were paddling out of the country in a Peterborough, and gave

him shelter for the night in their storm-bound
camp. Next morning they departed, but he
elected to stay by his eggs. And thereafter
the name and fame of the man with the thousand dozen eggs began to spread through the
land. Gold-seekers who made in before the
freeze-up carried the news of his coming.
Grizzled old-timers of Forty Mile and Circle
City, sour doughs with leathern jaws and bean-
calloused stomachs, called up dream memories
of chickens and green things at mention of
his name. Dyea and Skaguay took an interest
in his being, and questioned his progress from
every man who came over the passes, while
Dawson—golden, omeletless Dawson—fretted
and worried, and waylaid every chance arrival
for word of him.

But of this, Rasmunsen knew nothing. The
day after the wreck he patched up the *Alma*
and pulled out. A cruel east wind blew in his
teeth from Tagish, but he got the oars over
the side and bucked manfully into it, though
half the time he was drifting backward and
chopping ice from the blades. According to

the custom of the country, he was driven ashore at Windy Arm; three times on Tagish saw him swamped and beached; and Lake Marsh held him at the freeze-up. The *Alma* was crushed in the jamming of the floes, but the eggs were intact. These he back-tripped two miles across the ice to the shore, where he built a caché, which stood for years after and was pointed out by men who knew.

Half a thousand frozen miles stretched between him and Dawson, and the waterway was closed. But Rasmunsen, with a peculiar tense look in his face, struck back up the lakes on foot. What he suffered on that lone trip, with naught but a single blanket, an axe, and a handful of beans, is not given to ordinary mortals to know. Only the Arctic adventurer may understand. Suffice that he was caught in a blizzard on Chilkoot and left two of his toes with the surgeon at Sheep Camp. Yet he stood on his feet and washed dishes in the scullery of the *Pawona* to the Puget Sound, and from there passed coal on a P. S. boat to San Francisco.

It was a haggard, unkempt man who limped

across the shining office floor to raise a second
mortgage from the bank people. His hollow
cheeks betrayed themselves through the
scraggly beard, and his eyes seemed to have
retired into deep caverns where they burned
with cold fires. His hands were grained from
exposure and hard work, and the nails were
rimmed with tight-packed dirt and coal dust.
He spoke vaguely of eggs and ice-packs, winds
and tides; but when they declined to let him
have more than a second thousand, his talk
became incoherent, concerning itself chiefly
with the price of dogs and dog-food, and such
things as snowshoes and moccasins and winter
trails. They let him have fifteen hundred,
which was more than the cottage warranted,
and breathed easier when he scrawled his signature and passed out the door.

Two weeks later he went over Chilkoot with
three dog sleds of five dogs each. One team
he drove, the two Indians with him driving
the others. At Lake Marsh they broke out
the caché and loaded up. But there was no
trail. He was the first in over the ice, and to

him fell the task of packing the snow and hammering away through the rough river jams. Behind him he often observed a camp-fire smoke trickling thinly up through the quiet air, and he wondered why the people did not overtake him. For he was a stranger to the land and did not understand. Nor could he understand his Indians when they tried to explain. This they conceived to be a hardship, but when they balked and refused to break camp of mornings, he drove them to their work at pistol point.

When he slipped through an ice bridge near the White Horse and froze his foot, tender yet and oversensitive from the previous freezing, the Indians looked for him to lie up. But he sacrificed a blanket, and, with his foot incased in an enormous moccasin, big as a water-bucket, continued to take his regular turn with the front sled. Here was the cruelest work, and they respected him, though on the side they rapped their foreheads with their knuckles and significantly shook their heads. One night they tried to run away, but the zip-

zip of his bullets in the snow brought them back, snarling but convinced. Whereupon, being only savage Chilkat men, they put their heads together to kill him; but he slept like a cat, and, waking or sleeping, the chance never came. Often they tried to tell him the import of the smoke wreath in the rear, but he could not comprehend and grew suspicious of them. And when they sulked or shirked, he was quick to let drive at them between the eyes, and quick to cool their heated souls with sight of his ready revolver.

And so it went — with mutinous men, wild dogs, and a trail that broke the heart. He fought the men to stay with him, fought the dogs to keep them away from the eggs, fought the ice, the cold, and the pain of his foot, which would not heal. As fast as the young tissue renewed, it was bitten and seared by the frost, so that a running sore developed, into which he could almost shove his fist. In the mornings, when he first put his weight upon it, his head went dizzy, and he was near to fainting from the pain; but later on in the day it

usually grew numb, to recommence when he
crawled into his blankets and tried to sleep.
Yet he, who had been a clerk and sat at a desk
all his days, toiled till the Indians were exhausted, and even outworked the dogs.   How
hard he worked, how much he suffered, he did
not know.   Being a man of the one idea, now
that the idea had come, it mastered him.   In
the foreground of his consciousness was Dawson, in the background his thousand dozen
eggs, and midway between the two his ego
fluttered, striving alway to draw them together
to a glittering golden point.   This golden
point was the five thousand dollars, the con-
summation of the idea and the point of departure for whatever new idea might present
itself.   For the rest, he was a mere automaton.
He was unaware of other things, seeing them
as through a glass darkly, and giving them no
thought.   The work of his hands he did with
machine-like wisdom ; likewise the work of his
head.   So the look on his face grew very tense,
till even the Indians were afraid of it, and
marvelled at the strange white man who had

made them slaves and forced them to toil with such foolishness.

Then came a snap on Lake Le Barge, when the cold of outer space smote the tip of the planet, and the frost ranged sixty and odd degrees below zero. Here, laboring with open mouth that he might breathe more freely, he chilled his lungs, and for the rest of the trip he was troubled with a dry, hacking cough, especially irritable in smoke of camp or under stress of undue exertion. On the Thirty Mile river he found much open water, spanned by precarious ice bridges and fringed with narrow rim ice, tricky and uncertain. The rim ice was impossible to reckon on, and he dared it without reckoning, falling back on his revolver when his drivers demurred. But on the ice bridges, covered with snow though they were, precautions could be taken. These they crossed on their snowshoes, with long poles, held crosswise in their hands, to which to cling in case of accident. Once over, the dogs were called to follow. And on such a bridge, where the absence of the centre ice was masked by the snow, one of the Indians met his end. He went through as quickly and neatly as a knife through thin cream, and the current swept him from view down under the stream ice.

That night his mate fled away through the pale moonlight, Rasmunsen futilely puncturing the silence with his revolver — a thing that he handled with more celerity than cleverness. Thirty-six hours later the Indian made a police camp on the Big Salmon.

"Um — um — um funny mans — what you call? — top um head all loose," the interpreter explained to the puzzled captain. "Eh? Yep, clazy, much clazy mans. Eggs, eggs, all a time eggs — savvy? Come bime-by."

It was several days before Rasmunsen arrived, the three sleds lashed together, and all the dogs in a single team. It was awkward, and where the going was bad he was compelled to back-trip it sled by sled, though he managed most of the time, through herculean efforts, to bring all along on the one haul. He did not seem moved when the captain of police told him his man was hitting the high places for Dawson, and was by that time, probably, halfway between Selkirk and Stewart. Nor did he appear interested when informed that the police had broken the trail as far as Pelly; for he had attained to a fatalistic acceptance of all natural dispensations, good or ill. But when they told him that Dawson was in the bitter clutch of famine, he smiled, threw the harness on his dogs, and pulled out.

But it was at his next halt that the mystery of the smoke was explained. With the word at Big Salmon that the trail was broken to Pelly, there was no longer any need for the smoke wreath to linger in his wake; and Rasmunsen, crouching over his lonely fire, saw a motley string of sleds go by. First came the courier and the half-breed who had hauled him out from Bennett; then mail-carriers for Circle City, two sleds of them, and a mixed following of ingoing Klondikers. Dogs and men were fresh and fat, while Rasmunsen and his brutes were jaded and worn down to the skin and bone. They of the smoke wreath had travelled one day in three, resting and reserving their strength for the dash to come when broken trail was met with; while each day he had plunged and floundered forward, breaking the spirit of his dogs and robbing them of their mettle.

As for himself, he was unbreakable. They thanked him kindly for his efforts in their behalf, those fat, fresh men, — thanked him kindly, with broad grins and ribald laughter; and now, when he understood, he made no answer. Nor did he cherish silent bitterness. It was immaterial. The idea — the fact behind the idea — was not changed. Here he was and his thousand dozen; there was Dawson; the problem was unaltered.

At the Little Salmon, being short of dog food, the dogs got into his grub, and from there to Selkirk he lived on beans — coarse, brown beans, big beans, grossly nutritive, which griped his stomach and doubled him up at two-hour intervals. But the Factor at Selkirk had a notice on the door of the Post to the effect that no steamer had been up the Yukon for two years, and in consequence grub was beyond price. He offered to swap flour, however, at the rate of a cupful for each egg, but Rasmunsen shook his head and hit the trail. Below the Post he managed to buy frozen horse hide for the dogs, the horses having been slain by the Chilkat cattle men, and the scraps and offal preserved by the Indians. He tackled the hide himself, but the hair worked into the bean sores of his mouth, and was beyond endurance.

Here at Selkirk, he met the forerunners of the hungry exodus of Dawson, and from there on they crept over the trail, a dismal throng. "No grub!" was the song they sang. "No grub, and had to go." "Everybody holding candles for a rise in the spring." "Flour dollar'n a half a pound, and no sellers."

"Eggs?" one of them answered. "Dollar apiece, but they ain't none."

Rasmunsen made a rapid calculation. "Twelve thousand dollars," he said aloud.

"Hey?" the man asked.

"Nothing," he answered, and *mushed* the dogs along.

When he arrived at Stewart River, seventy miles from Dawson, five of his dogs were gone, and the remainder were falling in the traces. He, also, was in the traces, hauling with what little strength was left in him. Even then he was barely crawling along ten miles a day. His cheek-bones and nose, frost-bitten again and again, were turned bloody-black and hideous. The thumb, which was separated from the fingers by the gee-pole, had likewise been nipped and gave him great pain. The monstrous moccasin still incased his foot, and strange pains were beginning to rack the leg. At Sixty Mile, the last beans, which he had been rationing for some time, were finished; yet he steadfastly refused to touch the eggs. He could not reconcile his mind to the legitimacy of it, and staggered and fell along the way to Indian River. Here a fresh-killed moose and an open-handed old-timer gave him and his dogs new strength, and at Ainslie's he felt repaid for it all when a stampede, ripe from Dawson in five hours, was sure he could get a dollar and a quarter for every egg he possessed.

He came up the steep bank by the Dawson barracks with fluttering heart and shaking knees. The dogs were so weak that he was forced to rest them, and, waiting, he leaned limply against the gee-pole. A man, an eminently decorous-looking man, came sauntering by in a great bearskin coat. He glanced at Rasmunsen curiously, then stopped and ran a speculative eye over the dogs and the three lashed sleds.

" What you got ? " he asked.

" Eggs," Rasmunsen answered huskily, hardly able to pitch his voice above a whisper.

" Eggs ! Whoopee ! Whoopee ! " He sprang up into the air, gyrated madly, and finished with half a dozen war steps. " You don't say — all of 'em ? "

" All of 'em ? "

" Say, you must be the Egg Man." He walked around and viewed Rasmunsen from the other side. " Come, now, ain't you the Egg Man ? "

Rasmunsen didn't know, but supposed he was, and the man sobered down a bit.

" What d'ye expect to get for 'em ? " he asked cautiously.

Rasmunsen became audacious. " Dollar'n a half," he said.

" Done ! " the man came back promptly. " Gimme a dozen."

" I — I mean a dollar'n a half apiece," Rasmunsen hesitatingly explained.

" Sure. I heard you. Make it two dozen. Here's the dust."

The man pulled out a healthy gold sack the size of a small sausage and knocked it negligently against the gee-pole. Rasmunsen felt a strange trembling in the pit of his stomach, a tickling of the nostrils, and an almost overwhelming desire to sit down and cry. But a curious, wide-eyed crowd was beginning to collect, and man after man was calling out for eggs. He was without scales, but the man with the bearskin coat fetched a pair and

obligingly weighed in the dust while Rasmunsen passed out the goods. Soon there was a
pushing and shoving and shouldering, and a
great clamor. Everybody wanted to buy and
to be served first. And as the excitement
grew, Rasmunsen cooled down. This would
never do. There must be something behind
the fact of their buying so eagerly. It would
be wiser if he rested first and sized up the
market. Perhaps eggs were worth two dollars
apiece. Anyway, whenever he wished to sell,
he was sure of a dollar and a half. "Stop!"
he cried, when a couple of hundred had been
sold. "No more now. I'm played out. I've
got to get a cabin, and then you can come
and see me."

A groan went up at this, but the man
with the bearskin coat approved. Twenty-
four of the frozen eggs went rattling in his
capacious pockets and he didn't care whether
the rest of the town ate or not. Besides, he
could see Rasmunsen was on his last legs.

"There's a cabin right around the second
corner from the Monte Carlo," he told him —

"the one with the sody-bottle window. It ain't mine, but I've got charge of it. Rents for ten a day and cheap for the money. You move right in, and I'll see you later. Don't forget the sody-bottle window."

"Tra-la-loo!" he called back a moment later. "I'm goin' up the hill to eat eggs and dream of home."

On his way to the cabin, Rasmunsen recollected he was hungry and bought a small supply of provisions at the N. A. T. & T. store — also a beefsteak at the butcher shop and dried salmon for the dogs. He found the cabin without difficulty and left the dogs in the harness while he started the fire and got the coffee under way.

"A dollar'n a half apiece — one thousand dozen — eighteen thousand dollars!" He kept muttering it to himself, over and over, as he went about his work.

As he flopped the steak into the frying-pan the door opened. He turned. It was the man with the bearskin coat. He seemed to come in with determination, as though bound on some explicit errand, but as he looked at Rasmunsen an expression of perplexity came into his face.

" I say — now I say — " he began, then halted.

Rasmunsen wondered if he wanted the rent.

" I say, damn it, you know, them eggs is bad."

Rasmunsen staggered. He felt as though some one had struck him an astounding blow between the eyes. The walls of the cabin reeled and tilted up. He put out his hand to steady himself and rested it on the stove. The sharp pain and the smell of the burning flesh brought him back to himself.

" I see," he said slowly, fumbling in his pocket for the sack. " You want your money back."

" It ain't the money," the man said, "but hain't you got any eggs — good ? "

Rasmunsen shook his head. " You'd better take the money."

But the man refused and backed away.

"I'll come back," he said, "when you've taken stock, and get what's comin'."

Rasmunsen rolled the chopping-block into the cabin and carried in the eggs. He went about it quite calmly. He took up the hand-axe, and, one by one, chopped the eggs in half. These halves he examined carefully and let fall to the floor. At first he sampled from the different cases, then deliberately emptied one case at a time. The heap on the floor grew larger. The coffee boiled over and the smoke of the burning beefsteak filled the cabin. He chopped steadfastly and monotonously till the last case was finished.

Somebody knocked at the door, knocked again, and let himself in.

"What a mess!" he remarked, as he paused and surveyed the scene.

The severed eggs were beginning to thaw in the heat of the stove, and a miserable odor was growing stronger.

"Must a-happened on the steamer," he suggested.

Rasmunsen looked at him long and blankly.

"I'm Murray, Big Jim Murray, everybody knows me," the man volunteered. "I'm just hearin' your eggs is rotten, and I'm offerin' you two hundred for the batch. They ain't good as salmon, but still they're fair scoffin's for dogs."

Rasmunsen seemed turned to stone. He did not move. "You go to hell," he said passionlessly.

"Now just consider. I pride myself it's a decent price for a mess like that, and it's bet-ter'n nothin'. Two hundred. What you say?"

"You go to hell," Rasmunsen repeated softly, "and get out of here."

Murray gaped with a great awe, then went out carefully, backward, with his eyes fixed on the other's face.

Rasmunsen followed him out and turned the dogs loose. He threw them all the sal-mon he had bought, and coiled a sled-lashing up in his hand. Then he reëntered the cabin and drew the latch in after him. The smoke from the cindered steak made his eyes smart.

He stood on the bunk, passed the lashing over the ridge-pole, and measured the swing-off with his eye. It did not seem to satisfy, for he put the stool on the bunk and climbed upon the stool.. He drove a noose in the end of the lashing and slipped his head through. The other end he made fast. Then he kicked the stool out from under.

THE MARRIAGE OF LIT-LIT

THE MARRIAGE OF LIT–LIT

WHEN John Fox came into a country where whiskey freezes solid and may be used as a paper-weight for a large part of the year, he came without the ideals and illusions that usually hamper the progress of more delicately nurtured adventurers. Born and reared on the frontier fringe of the United States, he took with him into Canada a primitive cast of mind, an elemental simplicity and grip on things, as it were, that insured him immediate success in his new career. From a mere servant of the Hudson's Bay Company, driving a paddle with the voyageurs and carrying goods on his back across the portages, he swiftly rose to a Factorship and took charge of a trading post at Fort Angelus.

Here, because of his elemental simplicity,

he took to himself a native wife, and, by reason of the connubial bliss that followed, he escaped the unrest and vain longings that curse the days of more fastidious men, spoil their work, and conquer them in the end. He lived contentedly, was at single purposes with the business he was set there to do, and achieved a brilliant record in the service of the Company. About this time his wife died, was claimed by her people, and buried with savage circumstance in a tin trunk in the top of a tree.

Two sons she had borne him, and when the Company promoted him, he journeyed with them still deeper into the vastness of the Northwest Territory to a place called Sin Rock, where he took charge of a new post in a more important fur field. Here he spent several lonely and depressing months, eminently disgusted with the unprepossessing appearance of the Indian maidens, and greatly worried by his growing sons who stood in need of a mother's care. Then his eyes chanced upon Lit-lit.

"Lit-lit — well, she is Lit-lit," was the fashion in which he despairingly described her to his chief clerk, Alexander McLean.

McLean was too fresh from his Scottish upbringing — "not dry behind the ears yet," John Fox put it — to take to the marriage customs of the country. Nevertheless he was not averse to the Factor's imperilling his own immortal soul, and, especially, feeling an ominous attraction himself for Lit-lit, he was sombrely content to clinch his own soul's safety by seeing her married to the Factor.

Nor is it to be wondered that McLean's austere Scotch soul stood in danger of being thawed in the sunshine of Lit-lit's eyes. She was pretty, and slender, and willowy, without the massive face and temperamental stolidity of the average squaw. "Lit-lit," so called from her fashion, even as a child, of being fluttery, of darting about from place to place like a butterfly, of being inconsequent and merry, and of laughing as lightly as she darted and danced about.

Lit-lit was the daughter of Snettishane, a

prominent chief in the tribe, by a half-breed mother, and to him the Factor fared casually one summer day to open negotiations of marriage. He sat with the chief in the smoke of a mosquito smudge before his lodge, and together they talked about everything under the sun, or, at least, everything that in the Northland is under the sun, with the sole exception of marriage. John Fox had come particularly to talk of marriage; Snettishane knew it, and John Fox knew he knew it, wherefore the subject was religiously avoided. This is alleged to be Indian subtlety. In reality it is transparent simplicity.

The hours slipped by, and Fox and Snettishane smoked interminable pipes, looking each other in the eyes with a guilelessness superbly histrionic. In the mid-afternoon McLean and his brother clerk, McTavish, strolled past, innocently uninterested, on their way to the river. When they strolled back again an hour later, Fox and Snettishane had attained to a ceremonious discussion of the condition and quality of the gunpowder and bacon which the Company was offering in trade. Meanwhile Lit-lit, divining the Factor's errand, had crept in under the rear wall of the lodge and through the front flap was peeping out at the two logomachists by the mosquito smudge. She was flushed and happy-eyed, proud that no less a man than the Factor (who stood next to God in the Northland hierarchy) had singled her out, femininely curious to see at close range what manner of man he was. Sunglare on the ice, camp smoke, and weather beat had burned his face to a copper-brown, so that her father was as fair as he, while she was fairer. She was remotely glad of this, and more immediately glad that he was large and strong, though his great black beard half frightened her, it was so strange.

Being very young, she was unversed in the ways of men. Seventeen times she had seen the sun travel south and lose itself beyond the sky-line, and seventeen times she had seen it travel back again and ride the sky day and night till there was no night at all. And through these years she had been cherished jealously by Snettishane, who stood between her and all suitors, listening disdainfully to the young hunters as they bid for her hand, and turning them away as though she were beyond price.   Snettishane was mercenary.   Lit-lit was to him an investment.   She represented so much capital, from which he expected to receive, not a certain definite interest, but an incalculable interest.

And having thus been reared in a manner as near to that of the nunnery as tribal conditions would permit, it was with a great and maidenly anxiety that she peeped out at the man who had surely come for her, at the husband who was to teach her all that was yet unlearned of life, at the masterful being whose word was to be her law, and who was to mete and bound her actions and comportment for the rest of her days.

But, peeping through the front flap of the lodge, flushed and thrilling at the strange destiny reaching out for her, she grew disappointed as the day wore along, and the Factor and her father still talked pompously of matters

concerning other things and not pertaining
to marriage things at all. As the sun sank
lower and lower toward the north and midnight approached, the Factor began making
unmistakable preparations for departure. As
he turned to stride away Lit-lit's heart sank ;
but it rose again as he halted, half turning on
one heel.

"Oh, by the way, Snettishane," he said,
"I want a squaw to wash for me and mend
my clothes."

Snettishane grunted and suggested Wanidani, who was an old woman and toothless.

"No, no," interposed the Factor. "What
I want is a wife. I've been kind of thinking
about it, and the thought just struck me that
you might know of some one that would
suit."

Snettishane looked interested, whereupon
the Factor retraced his steps, casually and
carelessly to linger and discuss this new and
incidental topic.

"Kattou ?" suggested Snettishane.

"She has but one eye," objected the Factor.

"Laska?"

"Her knees be wide apart when she stands upright. Kips, your biggest dog, can leap between her knees when she stands upright."

"Senatee?" went on the imperturbable Snettishane.

But John Fox feigned anger, crying: "What foolishness be this? Am I old, that thou shouldst mate me with old women? Am I toothless? lame of leg? blind of eye? Or am I poor that no bright-eyed maiden may look with favor upon me? Behold! I am the Factor, both rich and great, a power in the land, whose speech makes men tremble and is obeyed!"

Snettishane was inwardly pleased, though his sphinxlike visage never relaxed. He was drawing the Factor, and making him break ground. Being a creature so elemental as to have room for but one idea at a time, Snettishane could pursue that one idea a greater distance than could John Fox. For John Fox, elemental as he was, was still complex enough to entertain several glimmering ideas at a time, which debarred him from pursuing the one as single-heartedly or as far as did the chief.

Snettishane calmly continued calling the roster of eligible maidens, which, name by name, as fast as uttered, were stamped ineligible by John Fox, with specified objections appended. Again he gave it up and started to return to the Fort. Snettishane watched him go, making no effort to stop him, but seeing him, in the end, stop himself.

"Come to think of it," the Factor remarked, "we both of us forgot Lit-lit. Now I wonder if she'll suit me?"

Snettishane met the suggestion with a mirthless face, behind the mask of which his soul grinned wide. It was a distinct victory. Had the Factor gone but one step farther, perforce Snettishane would himself have mentioned the name of Lit-lit, but—the Factor had not gone that one step farther.

The chief was non-committal concerning Lit-lit's suitability, till he drove the white man into taking the next step in order of procedure.

"Well," the Factor meditated aloud, "the

only way to find out is to make a try of it."
He raised his voice. "So I will give for Lit-
lit ten blankets and three pounds of tobacco
which is good tobacco."

Snettishane replied with a gesture which
seemed to say that all the blankets and tobacco
in all the world could not compensate him for
the loss of Lit-lit and her manifold virtues.
When pressed by the Factor to set a price, he
coolly placed it at five hundred blankets, ten
guns, fifty pounds of tobacco, twenty scarlet
cloths, ten bottles of rum, a music-box, and
lastly the good-will and best offices of the
Factor, with a place by his fire.

The Factor apparently suffered a stroke of
apoplexy, which stroke was successful in reduc-
ing the blankets to two hundred and in cutting
out the place by the fire — an unheard-of
condition in the marriages of white men with
the daughters of the soil. In the end, after
three hours more of chaffering, they came to an
agreement. For Lit-lit Snettishane was to receive one hundred blankets, five pounds of
tobacco, three guns, and a bottle of rum, good-

will and best offices included, which, according to John Fox, was ten blankets and a gun more than she was worth. And as he went home through the wee sma' hours, the three o'clock sun blazing in the due northeast, he was unpleasantly aware that Snettishane had bested him over the bargain.

Snettishane, tired and victorious, sought his bed, and discovered Lit-lit before she could escape from the lodge.

He grunted knowingly: " Thou hast seen. Thou hast heard. Wherefore it be plain to thee thy father's very great wisdom and understanding. I have made for thee a great match. Heed my words and walk in the way of my words, go when I say go, come when I bid thee come, and we shall grow fat with the wealth of this big white man who is a fool according to his bigness."

The next day no trading was done at the store. The Factor opened whiskey before breakfast to the delight of McLean and McTavish, gave his dogs double rations, and wore his best moccasins. Outside the Fort

preparations were under way for a *potlatch*.
Potlatch means "a giving," and John Fox's
intention was to signalize his marriage with
Lit-lit by a potlatch as generous as she was
good-looking.   In the afternoon the whole tribe
gathered to the feast.   Men, women, children,
and dogs gorged to repletion, nor was there
one person, even among the chance visitors
and stray hunters from other tribes, who
failed to receive some token of the bride-
groom's largess.

Lit-lit, tearfully shy and frightened, was
bedecked by her bearded husband with a new
calico dress, splendidly beaded moccasins, a
gorgeous silk handkerchief over her raven
hair, a purple scarf about her throat, brass ear-
rings and finger-rings, and a whole pint of
pinchbeck jewellery, including a Waterbury
watch.   Snettishane could scarce contain himself at the spectacle, but watching his chance
drew her aside from the feast.

" Not this night, nor the next night," he
began ponderously, " but in the nights to come,
when I shall call like a raven by the river

bank, it is for thee to rise up from thy big husband who is a fool and come to me.

"Nay, nay," he went on hastily, at sight of the dismay in her face at turning her back upon her wonderful new life. "For no sooner shall this happen than thy big husband who is a fool will come wailing to my lodge. Then it is for thee to wail likewise, claiming that this thing is not well, and that the other thing thou dost not like, and that to be the wife of the Factor is more than thou didst bargain for, only wilt thou be content with more blankets, and more tobacco, and more wealth of various sorts for thy poor old father Snettishane. Remember well, when I call in the night, like a raven, from the river bank."

Lit-lit nodded; for to disobey her father was a peril she knew well; and, furthermore, it was a little thing he asked, a short separation from the Factor, who would know only greater gladness at having her back. She returned to the feast, and, midnight being well at hand, the Factor sought her out and led her away to the Fort amid joking and out-

cry in which the squaws were especially
conspicuous.

Lit-lit quickly found that married life with
the head-man of a fort was even better than she
had dreamed. No longer did she have to fetch
wood and water and wait hand and foot upon
cantankerous menfolk. For the first time in
her life she could lie abed till breakfast was
on the table. And what a bed! — clean and
soft, and comfortable as no bed she had ever
known. And such food! Flour, cooked into
biscuits, hot-cakes and bread, three times a day
and every day, and all one wanted! Such
prodigality was hardly believable.

To add to her contentment, the Factor was
cunningly kind. He had buried one wife, and
he knew how to drive with a slack rein that
went firm only on occasion, and then went very
firm. "Lit-lit is boss of this place," he announced significantly at the table the morning
after the wedding. "What she says goes.
Understand?" And McLean and McTavish
understood. Also, they knew that the Factor
had a heavy hand.

But Lit-lit did not take advantage. Taking a leaf from the book of her husband, she at once assumed charge of his two growing sons, giving them added comforts and a measure of freedom like to that which he gave her. The two sons were loud in the praise of their new mother; McLean and McTavish lifted their voices; and the Factor bragged of the joys of matrimony till the story of her good behavior and her husband's satisfaction became the property of all the dwellers in the Sin Rock district.

Whereupon Snettishane, with visions of his incalculable interest keeping him awake of nights, thought it time to bestir himself. On the tenth night of her wedded life Lit-lit was awakened by the croaking of a raven, and she knew that Snettishane was waiting for her by the river bank. In her great happiness she had forgotten her pact, and now it came back to her with behind it all the childish terror of her father. For a time she lay in fear and trembling, loath to go, afraid to stay. But in the end the Factor won the silent victory, and

his kindness, plus his great muscles and
square jaw, nerved her to disregard Snettishane's call.

But in the morning she arose very much
afraid, and went about her duties in momen-
tary fear of her father's coming. As the day
wore along, however, she began to recover her
spirits. John Fox, soundly berating McLean
and McTavish for some petty dereliction of
duty, helped her to pluck up courage. She
tried not to let him go out of her sight, and
when she followed him into the huge caché
and saw him twirling and tossing great bales
around as though they were feather pillows,
she felt strengthened in her disobedience to
her father. Also (it was her first visit to the
warehouse, and Sin Rock was the chief dis-
tributing point to several chains of lesser posts),
she was astounded at the endlessness of the
wealth there stored away.

This sight, and the picture in her mind's
eye of the bare lodge of Snettishane, put all
doubts at rest. Yet she capped her convic-
tion by a brief word with one of her stepsons.

"White daddy good?" was what she asked,
and the boy answered that his father was the
best man he had ever known. That night
the raven croaked again. On the night following the croaking was more persistent. It
awoke the Factor, who tossed restlessly for a
while. Then he said aloud, "Damn that
raven," and Lit-lit laughed quietly under the
blankets.

In the morning, bright and early, Snettishane put in an ominous appearance, and was
set to breakfast in the kitchen with Wanidani.
He refused "squaw food," and a little later
bearded his son-in-law in the store where the
trading was done. Having learned, he said,
that his daughter was such a jewel, he had
come for more blankets, more tobacco, and
more guns — especially more guns. He had
certainly been cheated in her price, he held, and
he had come for justice. But the Factor had
neither blankets nor justice to spare. Whereupon he was informed that Snettishane had seen
the missionary at Three Forks, who had noti-
fied him that such marriages were not made

in heaven, and that it was his father's duty to demand his daughter back.

" I am good Christian man now," Snetti-shane concluded. " I want my Lit-lit to go to heaven."

The Factor's reply was short and to the point; for he directed his father-in-law to go to the heavenly antipodes, and by the scruff of the neck and the slack of the blanket pro-pelled him on that trail as far as the door.

But Snettishane sneaked around and in by the kitchen, cornering Lit-lit in the great living-room of the Fort.

" Mayhap thou didst sleep oversound last night when I called by the river bank," he began, glowering darkly.

" Nay, I was awake and heard." Her heart was beating as though it would choke her, but she went on steadily, " And the night before I was awake and heard, and yet again the night before."

And thereat, out of her great happiness and out of the fear that it might be taken from her, she launched into an original and glowing ad-

dress upon the status and rights of woman —
the first new-woman lecture delivered north of
Fifty-three.

But it fell on unheeding ears. Snettishane
was still in the dark ages. As she paused for
breath, he said threateningly, " To-night I
shall call again like the raven."

At this moment the Factor entered the
room and again helped Snettishane on his way
to the heavenly antipodes.

That night the raven croaked more per-
sistently than ever. Lit-lit, who was a light
sleeper, heard and smiled. John Fox tossed
restlessly. Then he awoke and tossed about
with greater restlessness. He grumbled and
snorted, swore under his breath and over his
breath, and finally flung out of bed. He groped
his way to the great living-room and from the
rack took down a loaded shot-gun — loaded with
bird shot, left therein by the careless McTavish.

The Factor crept carefully out of the Fort
and down to the river. The croaking had
ceased, but he stretched out in the long
grass and waited. The air seemed a chilly

balm, and the earth, after the heat of the day, now and again breathed soothingly against him. The Factor, gathered into the rhythm of it all, dozed off, with his head upon his arm, and slept.

Fifty yards away, head resting on knees, and with his back to John Fox, Snettishane likewise slept, gently conquered by the quietude of the night. An hour slipped by and then he awoke, and, without lifting his head, set the night vibrating with the hoarse gutturals of the raven call.

The Factor roused, not with the abrupt start of civilized man, but with the swift and comprehensive glide from sleep to waking of the savage. In the night light he made out a dark object in the midst of the grass and brought his gun to bear upon it. A second croak began to rise, and he pulled the trigger. The crickets ceased from their sing-song chant, the wild fowl from their squabbling, and the raven croak broke midmost and died away in gasping silence.

John Fox ran to the spot and reached

for the thing he had killed, but his fingers closed on a coarse mop of hair and he
turned Snettishane's face upward to the star-
light. He knew how a shot-gun scattered at
fifty yards, and he knew that he had peppered
Snettishane across the shoulders and in the
small of the back. And Snettishane knew
that he knew, but neither referred to it.

"What dost thou here?" the Factor demanded. "It were time old bones should
be in bed."

But Snettishane was stately in spite of the
bird shot burning under his skin.

"Old bones will not sleep," he said
solemnly. "I weep for my daughter, for
my daughter Lit-lit, who liveth and who yet
is dead, and who goeth without doubt to the
white man's hell."

"Weep henceforth on the far bank, beyond
earshot of the fort," said John Fox, turning
on his heel, "for the noise of thy weeping
is exceeding great and will not let one sleep
of nights."

"My heart is sore," Snettishane answered,

"and my days and nights be black with sorrow."

"As the raven is black," said John Fox.

"As the raven is black," Snettishane said.

Never again was the voice of the raven heard by the river bank. Lit-lit grows matronly day by day and is very happy. Also, there are sisters to the sons of John Fox's first wife who lies buried in a tree. Old Snettishane is no longer a visitor at the Fort, and spends long hours raising a thin, aged voice against the filial ingratitude of children in general and of his daughter Lit-lit in particular. His declining years are embittered by the knowledge that he was cheated, and even John Fox has withdrawn the assertion that the price for Lit-lit was too much by ten blankets and a gun.

BÂTARD

BÂTARD

BÂTARD was a devil. This was recognized throughout the Northland.
"Hell's Spawn" he was called by
many men, but his master, Black Leclère,
chose for him the shameful name "Bâtard."
Now Black Leclère was also a devil, and the
twain were well matched. There is a saying
that when two devils come together, hell
is to pay. This is to be expected, and this
certainly was to be expected when Bâtard and
Black Leclère came together. The first time
they met, Bâtard was a part-grown puppy,
lean and hungry, with bitter eyes; and
they met with snap and snarl, and wicked
looks, for Leclère's upper lip had a wolfish
way of lifting and showing the white, cruel
teeth. And it lifted then, and his eyes glinted
viciously, as he reached for Bâtard and dragged

him out from the squirming litter. It was
certain that they divined each other, for on the
instant Bâtard had buried his puppy fangs in
Leclère's hand, and Leclère, thumb and finger,
was coolly choking his young life out of him.

"*Sacredam*," the Frenchman said softly,
flirting the quick blood from his bitten hand
and gazing down on the little puppy choking
and gasping in the snow.

Leclère turned to John Hamlin, storekeeper
of the Sixty Mile Post. "Dat fo' w'at Ah
lak heem. 'Ow moch, eh, you, *M'sieu'*?
'Ow moch? Ah buy heem, now; Ah buy
heem queek."

And because he hated him with an exceeding bitter hate, Leclère bought Bâtard and gave
him his shameful name. And for five years
the twain adventured across the Northland,
from St. Michael's and the Yukon delta to
the head-reaches of the Pelly and even so far
as the Peace River, Athabasca, and the Great
Slave. And they acquired a reputation for
uncompromising wickedness, the like of which
never before attached itself to man and dog.

Bâtard did not know his father, — hence his name, — but, as John Hamlin knew, his father was a great gray timber wolf. But the mother of Bâtard, as he dimly remembered her, was snarling, bickering, obscene, husky, full-fronted and heavy-chested, with a malign eye, a cat-like grip on life, and a genius for trickery and evil. There was neither faith nor trust in her. Her treachery alone could be relied upon, and her wild-wood amours attested her general depravity. Much of evil and much of strength were there in these, Bâtard's pro-genitors, and, bone and flesh of their bone and flesh, he had inherited it all. And then came Black Leclère, to lay his heavy hand on the bit of pulsating puppy life, to press and prod and mould till it became a big bristling beast, acute in knavery, overspilling with hate, sinis-ter, malignant, diabolical. With a proper master Bâtard might have made an ordinary, fairly efficient sled-dog. He never got the chance: Leclère but confirmed him in his congenital iniquity.

The history of Bâtard and Leclère is a

history of war — of five cruel, relentless years,
of which their first meeting is fit summary.
To begin with, it was Leclère's fault, for he
hated with understanding and intelligence,
while the long-legged, ungainly puppy hated
only blindly, instinctively, without reason or
method.   At first there were no refinements of
cruelty (these were to come later), but simple
beatings and crude brutalities.   In one of
these Bâtard had an ear injured.   He never
regained control of the riven muscles, and
ever after the ear drooped limply down to
keep keen the memory of his tormentor.
And he never forgot.

His puppyhood was a period of foolish
rebellion.   He was always worsted, but he
fought back because it was his nature to fight
back.   And he was unconquerable.   Yelping
shrilly from the pain of lash and club, he
none the less contrived always to throw in the
defiant snarl, the bitter vindictive menace of his
soul which fetched without fail more blows
and beatings.   But his was his mother's tena-
cious grip on life.   Nothing could kill him.

He flourished under misfortune, grew fat with famine, and out of his terrible struggle for life developed a preternatural intelligence. His were the stealth and cunning of the husky, his mother, and the fierceness and valor of the wolf, his father.

Possibly it was because of his father that he never wailed. His puppy yelps passed with his lanky legs, so that he became grim and taciturn, quick to strike, slow to warn. He answered curse with snarl, and blow with snap, grinning the while his implacable hatred; but never again, under the extremest agony, did Leclère bring from him the cry of fear nor of pain. This unconquerableness but fanned Leclère's wrath and stirred him to greater deviltries.

Did Leclère give Bâtard half a fish and to his mates whole ones, Bâtard went forth to rob other dogs of their fish. Also he robbed cachés and expressed himself in a thousand rogueries, till he became a terror to all dogs and masters of dogs. Did Leclère beat Bâtard and fondle Babette, — Babette who was not half the worker he was, — why, Bâtard threw her down in the snow and broke her hind leg in his heavy jaws, so that Leclère was forced to shoot her. Likewise, in bloody battles, Bâtard mastered all his team-mates, set them the law of trail and forage, and made them live to the law he set.

In five years he heard but one kind word, received but one soft stroke of a hand, and then he did not know what manner of things they were. He leaped like the untamed thing he was, and his jaws were together in a flash. It was the missionary at Sunrise, a newcomer in the country, who spoke the kind word and gave the soft stroke of the hand. And for six months after, he wrote no letters home to the States, and the surgeon at McQuestion travelled two hundred miles on the ice to save him from blood-poisoning.

Men and dogs looked askance at Bâtard when he drifted into their camps and posts. The men greeted him with feet threateningly lifted for the kick, the dogs with bristling manes and bared fangs. Once a man did kick

Bâtard, and Bâtard, with quick wolf snap,
closed his jaws like a steel trap on the
man's calf and crunched down to the bone.
Whereat the man was determined to have his
life, only Black Leclère, with ominous eyes
and naked hunting-knife, stepped in between.
The killing of Bâtard — ah, *sacredam, that*
was a pleasure Leclère reserved for himself.
Some day it would happen, or else — bah!
who was to know? Anyway, the problem
would be solved.

For they had become problems to each
other. The very breath each drew was a
challenge and a menace to the other. Their
hate bound them together as love could never
bind. Leclère was bent on the coming of the
day when Bâtard should wilt in spirit and
cringe and whimper at his feet. And Bâtard
— Leclère knew what was in Bâtard's mind,
and more than once had read it in Bâtard's
eyes. And so clearly had he read, that when
Bâtard was at his back, he made it a point to
glance often over his shoulder.

Men marvelled when Leclère refused large

money for the dog. "Some day you'll kill
him and be out his price," said John Hamlin
once, when Bâtard lay panting in the snow
where Leclère had kicked him, and no one
knew whether his ribs were broken, and no
one dared look to see.

"Dat," said Leclère, dryly, "dat is my biz'-
ness, *M'sieu'*."

And the men marvelled that Bâtard did
not run away. They did not understand.
But Leclère understood. He was a man who
lived much in the open, beyond the sound of
human tongue, and he had learned the voices
of wind and storm, the sigh of night, the
whisper of dawn, the clash of day. In a dim
way he could hear the green things growing,
the running of the sap, the bursting of the bud.
And he knew the subtle speech of the things
that moved, of the rabbit in the snare, the
moody raven beating the air with hollow wing,
the baldface shuffling under the moon, the
wolf like a gray shadow gliding betwixt the
twilight and the dark. And to him Bâtard
spoke clear and direct. Full well he under-

stood why Bâtard did not run away, and he
looked more often over his shoulder.

When in anger, Bâtard was not nice to look
upon, and more than once had he leapt for
Leclère's throat, to be stretched quivering and
senseless in the snow, by the butt of the ever
ready dogwhip.   And so Bâtard learned to
bide his time.   When he reached his full
strength and prime of youth, he thought the
time had come.   He was broad-chested, power-
fully muscled, of far more than ordinary size,
and his neck from head to shoulders was a
mass of bristling hair — to all appearances
a full-blooded wolf.   Leclère was lying asleep
in his furs when Bâtard deemed the time to be
ripe.   He crept upon him stealthily, head low
to earth and lone ear laid back, with a feline
softness of tread.   Bâtard breathed gently, very
gently, and not till he was close at hand did
he raise his head.   He paused for a moment,
and looked at the bronzed bull throat, naked
and knotty, and swelling to a deep and steady
pulse.   The slaver dripped down his fangs
and slid off his tongue at the sight, and in

that moment he remembered his drooping ear,
his uncounted blows and prodigious wrongs,
and without a sound sprang on the sleeping
man.

Leclère awoke to the pang of the fangs in
his throat, and, perfect animal that he was,
he awoke clear-headed and with full comprehension. He closed on Bâtard's windpipe
with both his hands, and rolled out of his furs
to get his weight uppermost. But the thousands of Bâtard's ancestors had clung at the
throats of unnumbered moose and caribou and
dragged them down, and the wisdom of those
ancestors was his. When Leclère's weight
came on top of him, he drove his hind legs
upward and in, and clawed down chest and
abdomen, ripping and tearing through skin
and muscle. And when he felt the man's body
wince above him and lift, he worried and shook
at the man's throat. His team-mates closed
around in a snarling circle, and Bâtard, with
failing breath and fading sense, knew that their
jaws were hungry for him. But that did not
matter — it was the man, the man above him,

and he ripped and clawed, and shook and
worried, to the last ounce of his strength.   But
Leclère choked him with both his hands, till
Bâtard's chest heaved and writhed for the air
denied, and his eyes glazed and set, and his
jaws slowly loosened, and his tongue protruded
black and swollen.

"Eh? *Bon*, you devil!" Leclère gurgled,
mouth and throat clogged with his own blood,
as he shoved the dizzy dog from him.

And then Leclère cursed the other dogs
off as they fell upon Bâtard.   They drew back
into a wider circle, squatting alertly on their
haunches and licking their chops, the hair on
every neck bristling and erect.

Bâtard recovered quickly, and at sound of
Leclère's voice, tottered to his feet and swayed
weakly back and forth.

"A-h-ah! You beeg devil!" Leclère spluttered.   "Ah fix you; Ah fix you plentee, by
Gar!"

Bâtard, the air biting into his exhausted
lungs like wine, flashed full into the man's
face, his jaws missing and coming together

with a metallic clip. They rolled over and
over on the snow, Leclère striking madly with
his fists. Then they separated, face to face,
and circled back and forth before each other.
Leclère could have drawn his knife. His
rifle was at his feet. But the beast in him
was up and raging. He would do the thing
with his hands — and his teeth. Bâtard
sprang in, but Leclère knocked him over with
a blow of the fist, fell upon him, and buried
his teeth to the bone in the dog's shoulder.

It was a primordial setting and a primordial
scene, such as might have been in the savage
youth of the world. An open space in a dark
forest, a ring of grinning wolf-dogs, and in the
centre two beasts, locked in combat, snapping
and snarling, raging madly about, panting,
sobbing, cursing, straining, wild with passion,
in a fury of murder, ripping and tearing and
clawing in elemental brutishness.

But Leclère caught Bâtard behind the ear,
with a blow from his fist, knocking him over,
and, for the instant, stunning him. Then
Leclère leaped upon him with his feet, and

sprang up and down, striving to grind him into the earth. Both Bâtard's hind legs were broken ere Leclère ceased that he might catch breath.

"A-a-ah! A-a-ah!" he screamed, incapable of speech, shaking his fist, through sheer impotence of throat and larynx.

But Bâtard was indomitable. He lay there in a helpless welter, his lip feebly lifting and writhing to the snarl he had not the strength to utter. Leclère kicked him, and the tired jaws closed on the ankle, but could not break the skin.

Then Leclère picked up the whip and proceeded almost to cut him to pieces, at each stroke of the lash crying: "Dis taim Ah break you! Eh? By *Gar!* Ah break you!"

In the end, exhausted, fainting from loss of blood, he crumpled up and fell by his victim, and when the wolf-dogs closed in to take their vengeance, with his last consciousness dragged his body on top Bâtard to shield him from their fangs.

This occurred not far from Sunrise, and the

missionary, opening the door to Leclère a few
hours later, was surprised to note the absence
of Bâtard from the team.   Nor did his surprise
lessen when Leclère threw back the robes from
the sled, gathered Bâtard into his arms, and
staggered across the threshold.   It happened
that the surgeon of McQuestion, who was
something of a gadabout, was up on a gossip,
and between them they proceeded to repair
Leclère.

"*Merci, non,*" said he.   "Do you fix firs'
de dog.   To die?   *Non.*   Eet is not good.
Becos' heem Ah mus' yet break.   Dat fo'
w'at he mus' not die."

The surgeon called it a marvel, the missionary
a miracle, that Leclère pulled through at all; and
so weakened was he, that in the spring the fever
got him, and he went on his back again.   Bâtard
had been in even worse plight, but his grip
on life prevailed, and the bones of his hind
legs knit, and his organs righted themselves,
during the several weeks he lay strapped to
the floor.   And by the time Leclère, finally
convalescent, sallow and shaky, took the sun

by the cabin door, Bâtard had reasserted his
supremacy among his kind, and brought not
only his own team-mates but the missionary's
dogs into subjection.

He moved never a muscle, nor twitched a
hair, when, for the first time, Leclère tottered
out on the missionary's arm, and sank down
slowly and with infinite caution on the three-
legged stool.

"*Bon!*" he said. "*Bon!* De good sun!"
And he stretched out his wasted hands and
washed them in the warmth.

Then his gaze fell on the dog, and the old
light blazed back in his eyes. He touched
the missionary lightly on the arm. "*Mon
père*, dat is one beeg devil, dat Bâtard. You
will bring me one pistol, so, dat Ah drink de
sun in peace."

And thenceforth for many days he sat in
the sun before the cabin door. He never
dozed, and the pistol lay always across his
knees. Bâtard had a way, the first thing each
day, of looking for the weapon in its wonted
place. At sight of it he would lift his lip

faintly in token that he understood, and
Leclère would lift his own lip in an answering
grin. One day the missionary took note of
the trick.

"Bless me!" he said. "I really believe
the brute comprehends."

Leclère laughed softly. "Look you, *mon
père*. Dat w'at Ah now spik, to dat does he
lissen."

As if in confirmation, Bâtard just perceptibly
wriggled his lone ear up to catch the sound.

"Ah say ' keel.' "

Bâtard growled deep down in his throat, the
hair bristled along his neck, and every muscle
went tense and expectant.

"Ah lift de gun, so, like dat." And suit-
ing action to word, he sighted the pistol at
Bâtard.

Bâtard, with a single leap, sideways, landed
around the corner of the cabin out of sight.

"Bless me!" he repeated at intervals.

Leclère grinned proudly.

"But why does he not run away?"

The Frenchman's shoulders went up in the

racial shrug that means all things from total
ignorance to infinite understanding.

"Then why do you not kill him?"

Again the shoulders went up.

"*Mon père*," he said after a pause, "de
taim is not yet. He is one beeg devil. Some
taim Ah break heem, so, an' so, all to leetle
bits. Hey? Some taim. *Bon!*"

A day came when Leclère gathered his
dogs together and floated down in a bateau
to Forty Mile, and on to the Porcupine, where
he took a commission from the P. C. Company, and went exploring for the better part
of a year. After that he poled up the Koyokuk to deserted Arctic City, and later came
drifting back, from camp to camp, along the
Yukon. And during the long months Bâtard
was well lessoned. He learned many tortures,
and, notably, the torture of hunger, the torture
of thirst, the torture of fire, and, worst of all,
the torture of music.

Like the rest of his kind, he did not enjoy
music. It gave him exquisite anguish, racking
him nerve by nerve, and ripping apart every

fibre of his being. It made him howl, long
and wolf-like, as when the wolves bay the stars
on frosty nights. He could not help howling.
It was his one weakness in the contest with
Leclère, and it was his shame. Leclère, on
the other hand, passionately loved music — as
passionately as he loved strong drink. And
when his soul clamored for expression, it usually uttered itself in one or the other of the
two ways, and more usually in both ways.
And when he had drunk, his brain a-lilt with
unsung song and the devil in him aroused and
rampant, his soul found its supreme utterance
in torturing Bâtard.

"Now we will haf a leetle museek,"
he would say. "Eh? W'at you t'ink,
Bâtard?"

It was only an old and battered harmonica,
tenderly treasured and patiently repaired; but
it was the best that money could buy, and out
of its silver reeds he drew weird vagrant airs
that men had never heard before. Then
Bâtard, dumb of throat, with teeth tight
clenched, would back away, inch by inch, to

the farthest cabin corner. And Leclère, playing, playing, a stout club tucked under his
arm, followed the animal up, inch by inch,
step by step, till there was no further retreat.

At first Bâtard would crowd himself into
the smallest possible space, grovelling close to
the floor; but as the music came nearer and
nearer, he was forced to uprear, his back
jammed into the logs, his fore legs fanning the
air as though to beat off the rippling waves of
sound. He still kept his teeth together, but
severe muscular contractions attacked his body,
strange twitchings and jerkings, till he was all
a-quiver and writhing in silent torment. As he
lost control, his jaws spasmodically wrenched
apart, and deep throaty vibrations issued forth,
too low in the register of sound for human ear
to catch. And then, nostrils distended, eyes
dilated, hair bristling in helpless rage, arose
the long wolf howl. It came with a slurring
rush upward, swelling to a great heart-break-
ing burst of sound, and dying away in sadly
cadenced woe — then the next rush upward,
octave upon octave; the bursting heart; and

the infinite sorrow and misery, fainting, fading,
falling, and dying slowly away.

It was fit for hell.   And Leclère, with fiendish ken, seemed to divine each particular nerve
and heartstring, and with long wails and trem-
blings and sobbing minors to make it yield up
its last shred of grief.   It was frightful, and
for twenty-four hours after, Bâtard was nervous
and unstrung, starting at common sounds, trip-
ping over his own shadow, but, withal, vicious
and masterful with his team-mates.   Nor did
he show signs of a breaking spirit.   Rather
did he grow more grim and taciturn, biding
his time with an inscrutable patience that
began to puzzle and weigh upon Leclère.
The dog would lie in the firelight, motionless,
for hours, gazing straight before him at Leclère,
and hating him with his bitter eyes.

Often the man felt that he had bucked
against the very essence of life — the unconquerable essence that swept the hawk down
out of the sky like a feathered thunderbolt,
that drove the great gray goose across the
zones, that hurled the spawning salmon

through two thousand miles of boiling Yukon flood. At such times he felt impelled to express his own unconquerable essence; and with strong drink, wild music, and Bâtard, he indulged in vast orgies, wherein he pitted his puny strength in the face of things, and challenged all that was, and had been, and was yet to be.

"Dere is somet'ing dere," he affirmed, when the rhythmed vagaries of his mind touched the secret chords of Bâtard's being and brought forth the long lugubrious howl. "Ah pool eet out wid bot' my han's, so, an' so. Ha! Ha! Eet is fonee! Eet is ver' fonee! De priest chant, de womans pray, de mans swear, de leetle bird go *peep-peep*, Bâtard, heem go *yow-yow* — an' eet is all de ver' same t'ing. Ha! Ha!"

Father Gautier, a worthy priest, once reproved him with instances of concrete perdition. He never reproved him again.

"Eet may be so, *mon père*," he made answer. "An' Ah t'ink Ah go troo hell a-snappin', lak de hemlock troo de fire. Eh, *mon père*?"

But all bad things come to an end as well as good, and so with Black Leclère. On the summer low water, in a poling boat, he left McDougall for Sunrise. He left McDougall in company with Timothy Brown, and arrived at Sunrise by himself. Further, it was known that they had quarrelled just previous to pulling out; for the *Lizzie*, a wheezy ten-ton sternwheeler, twenty-four hours behind, beat Leclère in by three days. And when he did get in, it was with a clean-drilled bullet-hole through his shoulder muscle, and a tale of ambush and murder.

A strike had been made at Sunrise, and things had changed considerably. With the infusion of several hundred gold-seekers, a deal of whiskey, and half a dozen equipped gamblers, the missionary had seen the page of his years of labor with the Indians wiped clean. When the squaws became preoccupied with cooking beans and keeping the fire going for the wifeless miners, and the bucks with swapping their warm furs for black bottles and broken timepieces, he took to his bed,

said "bless me" several times, and departed
to his final accounting in a rough-hewn, oblong
box. Whereupon the gamblers moved their
roulette and faro tables into the mission house,
and the click of chips and clink of glasses
went up from dawn till dark and to dawn
again.

Now Timothy Brown was well beloved
among these adventurers of the north. The
one thing against him was his quick temper
and ready fist, — a little thing, for which his
kind heart and forgiving hand more than
atoned. On the other hand, there was nothing to atone for Black Leclère. He was
"black," as more than one remembered deed
bore witness, while he was as well hated as
the other was beloved. So the men of Sunrise put an antiseptic dressing on his shoulder
and haled him before Judge Lynch.

It was a simple affair. He had quarrelled
with Timothy Brown at McDougall. With
Timothy Brown he had left McDougall.
Without Timothy Brown he had arrived at
Sunrise. Considered in the light of his evil-

ness, the unanimous conclusion was that he
had killed Timothy Brown. On the other
hand, Leclère acknowledged their facts, but
challenged their conclusion, and gave his own
explanation. Twenty miles out of Sunrise
he and Timothy Brown were poling the boat
along the rocky shore. From that shore two
rifle-shots rang out. Timothy Brown pitched
out of the boat and went down bubbling red,
and that was the last of Timothy Brown.
He, Leclère, pitched into the bottom of the
boat with a stinging shoulder. He lay very
quiet, peeping at the shore. After a time
two Indians stuck up their heads and came
out to the water's edge, carrying between them
a birch-bark canoe. As they launched it,
Leclère let fly. He potted one, who went
over the side after the manner of Timothy
Brown. The other dropped into the bottom
of the canoe, and then canoe and poling boat
went down the stream in a drifting battle.
After that they hung up on a split current,
and the canoe passed on one side of an island,
the poling boat on the other. That was the

last of the canoe, and he came on into Sunrise. Yes, from the way the Indian in the canoe jumped, he was sure he had potted him. That was all.

This explanation was not deemed adequate. They gave him ten hours' grace while the *Lizzie* steamed down to investigate. Ten hours later she came wheezing back to Sunrise. There had been nothing to investigate. No evidence had been found to back up his statements. They told him to make his will, for he possessed a fifty-thousand-dollar Sunrise claim, and they were a law-abiding as well as a law-giving breed.

Leclère shrugged his shoulders. " Bot one t'ing," he said; "a leetle, w'at you call, favor — a leetle favor, dat is eet. I gif my feefty t'ousan' dollair to de church. I gif my husky dog, Bâtard, to de devil. De leetle favor? Firs' you hang heem, an' den you hang me. Eet is good, eh?"

Good it was, they agreed, that Hell's Spawn should break trail for his master across the last divide, and the court was adjourned down

to the river bank, where a big spruce tree stood
by itself. Slackwater Charley put a hangman's
knot in the end of a hauling-line, and the noose
was slipped over Leclère's head and pulled
tight around his neck. His hands were tied
behind his back, and he was assisted to the top
of a cracker box. Then the running end of
the line was passed over an overhanging
branch, drawn taut, and made fast. To kick
the box out from under would leave him dancing on the air.

"Now for the dog," said Webster Shaw,
sometime mining engineer. "You'll have to
rope him, Slackwater."

Leclère grinned. Slackwater took a chew of
tobacco, rove a running noose, and proceeded
leisurely to coil a few turns in his hand. He
paused once or twice to brush particularly
offensive mosquitoes from off his face. Everybody was brushing mosquitoes, except Leclère,
about whose head a small cloud was visible.
Even Bâtard, lying full-stretched on the
ground, with his fore paws rubbed the pests
away from eyes and mouth.

But while Slackwater waited for Bâtard to lift his head, a faint call came down the quiet air, and a man was seen waving his arms and running across the flat from Sunrise. It was the storekeeper.

"C-call 'er off, boys," he panted, as he came in among them.

"Little Sandy and Bernadotte's jes' got in," he explained with returning breath. "Landed down below an' come up by the short cut. Got the Beaver with 'm. Picked 'm up in his canoe, stuck in a back channel, with a couple of bullet holes in 'm. Other buck was Klok-Kutz, the one that knocked spots out of his squaw and dusted."

"Eh? W'at Ah say? Eh?" Leclère cried exultantly. "Dat de one fo' sure! Ah know. Ah spik true."

"The thing to do is teach these damned Siwashes a little manners," spoke Webster Shaw. "They're getting fat and sassy, and we'll have to bring them down a peg. Round in all the bucks and string up the Beaver for an object lesson. That's the programme.

Come on and let's see what he's got to say for himself."

"Heh, M'sieu'!" Leclère called, as the crowd began to melt away through the twilight in the direction of Sunrise. "Ah lak ver' moch to see de fon."

"Oh, we'll turn you loose when we come back," Webster Shaw shouted over his shoulder. "In the meantime meditate on your sins and the ways of providence. It will do you good, so be grateful."

As is the way with men who are accustomed to great hazards, whose nerves are healthy and trained to patience, so it was with Leclère, who settled himself to the long wait — which is to say that he reconciled his mind to it. There was no settling of the body, for the taut rope forced him to stand rigidly erect. The least relaxation of the leg muscles pressed the rough-fibred noose into his neck, while the upright position caused him much pain in his wounded shoulder. He projected his under lip and expelled his breath upward along his face to blow the mosquitoes away from his eyes. But the situation had its compensation. To be snatched from the maw of death was well worth a little bodily suffering, only it was unfortunate that he should miss the hanging of the Beaver.

And so he mused, till his eyes chanced to fall upon Bâtard, head between fore paws and stretched on the ground asleep. And then Leclère ceased to muse. He studied the animal closely, striving to sense if the sleep were real or feigned. Bâtard's sides were heaving regularly, but Leclère felt that the breath came and went a shade too quickly; also he felt that there was a vigilance or alertness to every hair that belied unshackling sleep. He would have given his Sunrise claim to be assured that the dog was not awake, and once, when one of his joints cracked, he looked quickly and guiltily at Bâtard to see if he roused. He did not rouse then, but a few minutes later he got up slowly and lazily, stretched, and looked carefully about him.

"*Sacredam*," said Leclère, under his breath. Assured that no one was in sight or hearing,

Bâtard sat down, curled his upper lip almost
into a smile, looked up at Leclère, and licked
his chops.

"Ah see my feenish," the man said, and
laughed sardonically aloud.

Bâtard came nearer, the useless ear wabbling,
the good ear cocked forward with devilish
comprehension.   He thrust his head on one
side quizzically, and advanced with mincing,
playful steps.   He rubbed his body gently
against the box till it shook and shook again.
Leclère teetered carefully to maintain his
equilibrium.

"Bâtard," he said calmly, "look out.   Ah
keel you."

Bâtard snarled at the word, and shook the
box with greater force.   Then he upreared,
and with his fore paws threw his weight against
it higher up.   Leclère kicked out with one foot,
but the rope bit into his neck and checked so
abruptly as nearly to overbalance him.

"Hi, ya! *Chook! Mush-on!*" he screamed.

Bâtard retreated, for twenty feet or so, with
a fiendish levity in his bearing that Leclère

could not mistake. He remembered the dog
often breaking the scum of ice on the water
hole, by lifting up and throwing his weight
upon it; and, remembering, he understood
what he now had in mind. Bâtard faced
about and paused. He showed his white
teeth in a grin, which Leclère answered; and
then hurled his body through the air, in full
charge, straight for the box.

Fifteen minutes later, Slackwater Charley
and Webster Shaw, returning, caught a glimpse
of a ghostly pendulum swinging back and
forth in the dim light. As they hurriedly
drew in closer, they made out the man's inert
body, and a live thing that clung to it, and
shook and worried, and gave to it the swaying motion.

"Hi, ya! *Chook!* you Spawn of Hell,"
yelled Webster Shaw.

But Bâtard glared at him, and snarled
threateningly, without loosing his jaws.

Slackwater Charley got out his revolver,
but his hand was shaking, as with a chill, and
he fumbled.

"Here, you take it," he said, passing the weapon over.

Webster Shaw laughed shortly, drew a sight between the gleaming eyes, and pressed the trigger. Bâtard's body twitched with the shock, threshed the ground spasmodically for a moment, and went suddenly limp. But his teeth still held fast locked.

THE STORY OF JEES UCK

THE STORY OF JEES UCK

THERE have been renunciations, and renunciations. But, in its essence, renunciation is ever the same. And the paradox of it is that men and women forego the dearest thing in the world for something dearer. It was never otherwise. Thus it was when Abel brought of the firstlings of his flock and of the fat thereof. The firstlings and the fat thereof were to him the dearest things in the world; yet he gave them over that he might be on good terms with God. So it was with Abraham when he prepared to offer up his son Isaac on a stone. Isaac was very dear to him; but God, in incomprehensible ways, was yet dearer. It may be that Abraham feared the Lord. But whether that be true or not, it has since been determined by a few billion people that he loved the Lord and desired to serve Him.

And since it has been determined that love is service, and since to renounce is to serve, then Jees Uck, who was merely a woman of a swart-skinned breed, loved with a great love. She was unversed in history, having learned to read only the signs of weather and of game; so she had never heard of Abel, nor of Abraham; nor, having escaped the good sisters at Holy Cross, had she been told the story of Ruth, the Moabitess, who renounced her very God for the sake of a stranger woman from a strange land. Jees Uck had learned only one way of renouncing, and that was with a club as the dynamic factor, in much the same manner as a dog is made to renounce a stolen marrow-bone. Yet, when the time came, she proved herself capable of rising to the height of the fair-faced royal races and of renouncing in right regal fashion.

So this is the story of Jees Uck, which is also the story of Neil Bonner, and Kitty Bonner, and a couple of Neil Bonner's progeny. Jees Uck was of a swart-skinned breed, it is true, but she was not an Indian;

nor was she an Eskimo; nor even an Innuit. Going backward into mouth tradition, there appears the figure of one Skolkz, a Toyaat Indian of the Yukon, who journeyed down in his youth to the Great Delta where dwell the Innuits, and where he forgathered with a woman remembered as Olillie. Now the woman Olillie had been bred from an Eskimo mother by an Innuit man. And from Skolkz and Olillie came Halie, who was one-half Toyaat Indian, one-quarter Innuit, and one-quarter Eskimo. And Halie was the grand-mother of Jees Uck.

Now Halie, in whom three stocks had been bastardized, who cherished no prejudice against further admixture, mated with a Russian fur trader called Shpack, also known in his time as the Big Fat. Shpack is herein classed Russian for lack of a more adequate term; for Shpack's father, a Slavonic convict from the Lower Provinces, had escaped from the quick-silver mines into Northern Siberia, where he knew Zimba, who was a woman of the Deer People and who became the mother of

Shpack, who became the grandfather of Jees Uck.

Now had not Shpack been captured in his boyhood by the Sea People, who fringe the rim of the Arctic Sea with their misery, he would not have become the grandfather of Jees Uck and there would be no story at all. But he *was* captured by the Sea People, from whom he escaped to Kamchatka, and thence, on a Norwegian whale-ship, to the Baltic. Not long after that he turned up in St. Petersburg, and the years were not many till he went drifting east over the same weary road his father had measured with blood and groans a half-century before. But Shpack was a free man, in the employ of the great Russian Fur Company. And in that employ he fared farther and farther east, until he crossed Bering Sea into Russian America; and at Pastolik, which is hard by the Great Delta of the Yukon, became the husband of Halie, who was the grandmother of Jees Uck. Out of this union came the woman-child, Tukesan.

Shpack, under the orders of the company, made a canoe voyage of a few hundred miles up the Yukon to the post of Nulato. With him he took Halie and the babe Tukesan. This was in 1850, and in 1850 it was that the river Indians fell upon Nulato and wiped it from the face of the earth. And that was the end of Shpack and Halie. On that terrible night Tukesan disappeared. To this day the Toyaats aver they had no hand in the trouble; but, be that as it may, the fact remains that the babe Tukesan grew up among them.

Tukesan was married successively to two Toyaat brothers, to both of whom she was barren. Because of this, other women shook their heads, and no third Toyaat man could be found to dare matrimony with the childless widow. But at this time, many hundred miles above, at Fort Yukon, was a man, Spike O'Brien. Fort Yukon was a Hudson Bay Company post, and Spike O'Brien one of the company's servants. He was a good servant, but he achieved an opinion that the service

was bad, and in the course of time vindicated
that opinion by deserting.   It was a year's
journey, by the chain of posts, back to York
Factory on Hudson's Bay.   Further, being
company posts, he knew he could not evade
the company's clutches.   Nothing remained
but to go down the Yukon.   It was true no
white man had ever gone down the Yukon,
and no white man knew whether the Yukon
emptied into the Arctic Ocean or Bering Sea ;
but Spike O'Brien was a Celt, and the promise of danger was a lure he had ever followed.

A few weeks later, somewhat battered,
rather famished, and about dead with river-
fever, he drove the nose of his canoe into
the earth bank by the village of the Toyaats
and promptly fainted away.   While getting
his strength back, in the weeks that followed,
he looked upon Tukesan and found her good.
Like the father of Shpack, who lived to a
ripe old age among the Siberian Deer People,
Spike O'Brien might have left his aged bones
with the Toyaats.   But romance gripped his
heart-strings and would not let him stay.   As

he had journeyed from York Factory to Fort
Yukon, so, first among men, might he journey
from Fort Yukon to the sea and win the honor
of being the first man to make the Northwest
Passage by land.   So he departed down the
river, won the honor, and was unannaled and
unsung.   In after years he ran a sailors' board-
ing-house in San Francisco, where he became
esteemed a most remarkable liar by virtue
of the gospel truths he told.   But a child
was born to Tukesan, who had been childless.
And this child was Jees Uck.   Her lineage
has been traced at length to show that she
was neither Indian, nor Eskimo, nor Innuit,
nor much of anything else; also to show
what waifs of the generations we are, all of
us, and the strange meanderings of the seed
from which we spring.

What with the vagrant blood in her and
the heritage compounded of many races, Jees
Uck developed a wonderful young beauty.
Bizarre, perhaps, it was, and Oriental enough
to puzzle any passing ethnologist.   A lithe
and slender grace characterized her.   Beyond

a quickened lilt to the imagination, the contribution of the Celt was in no wise apparent. It might possibly have put the warm blood under her skin, which made her face less swart and her body fairer; but that, in turn, might have come from Shpack, the Big Fat, who inherited the color of his Slavonic father. And, finally, she had great, blazing black eyes — the half-caste eye, round, full-orbed, and sensuous, which marks the collision of the dark races with the light.   Also, the white blood in her, combined with her knowledge that it was in her, made her, in a way, ambitious.   Otherwise, by upbringing and in outlook on life, she was wholly and utterly a Toyaat Indian.

One winter, when she was a young woman, Neil Bonner came into her life.   But he came into her life, as he had come into the country, somewhat reluctantly.   In fact, it was very much against his will, coming into the country. Between a father who clipped coupons and cultivated roses, and a mother who loved the social round, Neil Bonner had gone rather wild.   He was not vicious, but a man with meat in his belly and without work in the world has to expend his energy somehow, and Neil Bonner was such a man.   And he expended his energy in such fashion and to such extent that when the inevitable climax came, his father, Neil Bonner, senior, crawled out of his roses in a panic and looked on his son with a wondering eye.   Then he hied himself away to a crony of kindred pursuits, with whom he was wont to confer over coupons and roses, and between the two the destiny of young Neil Bonner was made manifest.   He must go away, on probation, to live down his harmless follies in order that he might live up to their own excellent standard.

This determined upon, and young Neil a little repentant and a great deal ashamed, the rest was easy.   The cronies were heavy stockholders in the P. C. Company.   The P. C. Company owned fleets of river-steamers and ocean-going craft, and, in addition to farming the sea, exploited a hundred thousand square miles or so of the land that, on the maps of geographers, usually occupies the white spaces. So the P. C. Company sent young Neil Bonner north, where the white spaces are, to do its work and to learn to be good like his father. "Five years of simplicity, close to the soil and far from temptation, will make a man of him," said old Neil Bonner, and forthwith crawled back among his roses. Young Neil set his jaw, pitched his chin at the proper angle, and went to work. As an underling he did his work well and gained the commendation of his superiors. Not that he delighted in the work, but that it was the one thing that prevented him from going mad.

The first year he wished he was dead. The second year he cursed God. The third year he was divided between the two emotions, and in the confusion quarrelled with a man in authority. He had the best of the quarrel, though the man in authority had the last word, —a word that sent Neil Bonner into an exile that made his old billet appear as paradise. But he went without a whimper, for the North had succeeded in making him into a man.

Here and there, on the white spaces on the map, little circlets like the letter " o " are to be found, and, appended to these circlets, on one side or the other, are names such as " Fort Hamilton," "Yanana Station," "Twenty Mile," thus leading one to imagine that the white spaces are plentifully besprinkled with towns and villages. But it is a vain imagining. Twenty Mile, which is very like the rest of the posts, is a log building the size of a corner grocery with rooms to let upstairs. A long-legged caché on stilts may be found in the back yard; also a couple of outhouses. The back yard is unfenced, and extends to the sky-line and an unascertainable bit beyond. There are no other houses in sight, though the Toyaats sometimes pitch a winter camp a mile or two down the Yukon. And this is Twenty Mile, one tentacle of the many-tentacled P. C. Company. Here the agent, with an assistant, barters with the Indians for their furs, and does an erratic trade on a gold-dust basis with the wandering miners. Here, also, the agent and his assistant yearn all winter for the spring,

and when the spring comes, camp blasphe-
mously on the roof while the Yukon washes
out the establishment. And here, also, in the
fourth year of his sojourn in the land, came
Neil Bonner to take charge.

He had displaced no agent; for the man
that previously ran the post had made away
with himself; "because of the rigors of the
place," said the assistant, who still remained;
though the Toyaats, by their fires, had another
version. The assistant was a shrunken-shoul-
dered, hollow-chested man, with a cadaverous
face and cavernous cheeks that his sparse
black beard could not hide. He coughed
much, as though consumption gripped his
lungs, while his eyes had that mad, fevered
light common to consumptives in the last
stage. Pentley was his name, — Amos Pentley, — and Bonner did not like him, though he
felt a pity for the forlorn and hopeless devil.
They did not get along together, these two
men who, of all men, should have been on
good terms in the face of the cold and silence
and darkness of the long winter.

In the end, Bonner concluded that Amos was partly demented, and left him alone, doing all the work himself except the cooking. Even then, Amos had nothing but bitter looks and an undisguised hatred for him. This was a great loss to Bonner; for the smiling face of one of his own kind, the cheery word, the sympathy of comradeship shared with misfortune — these things meant much; and the winter was yet young when he began to realize the added reasons, with such an assistant, that the previous agent had found to impel his own hand against his life.

It was very lonely at Twenty Mile. The bleak vastness stretched away on every side to the horizon. The snow, which was really frost, flung its mantle over the land and buried everything in the silence of death. For days it was clear and cold, the thermometer steadily recording forty to fifty degrees below zero. Then a change came over the face of things. What little moisture had oozed into the atmosphere gathered into dull gray, formless clouds; it became quite warm, the thermometer rising to twenty below; and the moisture fell out of the sky in hard frost-granules that hissed like dry sugar or driving sand when kicked underfoot. After that it became clear and cold again, until enough moisture had gathered to blanket the earth from the cold of outer space. That was all. Nothing happened. No storms, no churning waters and threshing forests, nothing but the machine-like precipitation of accumulated moisture. Possibly the most notable thing that occurred through the weary weeks was the gliding of the temperature up to the unprecedented height of fifteen below. To atone for this, outer space smote the earth with its cold till the mercury froze and the spirit thermometer remained more than seventy below for a fortnight, when it burst. There was no telling how much colder it was after that. Another occurrence, monotonous in its regularity, was the lengthening of the nights, till day became a mere blink of light between the darknesses.

Neil Bonner was a social animal. The very follies for which he was doing penance had been bred of his excessive sociability. And here, in the fourth year of his exile, he found himself in company — which were to travesty the word — with a morose and speechless creature in whose sombre eyes smouldered a hatred as bitter as it was unwarranted. And Bonner, to whom speech and fellowship were as the breath of life, went about as a ghost might go, tantalized by the gregarious revelries of some former life. In the day his lips were compressed, his face stern; but in the night he clenched his hands, rolled about in his blankets, and cried aloud like a little child. And he would remember a certain man in authority and curse him through the long hours. Also, he cursed God. But God understands. He cannot find it in His heart to blame weak mortals who blaspheme in Alaska.

And here, to the post of Twenty Mile, came Jees Uck, to trade for flour and bacon, and beads, and bright scarlet cloths for her fancy work. And further, and unwittingly, she came to the post of Twenty Mile to make a lonely man more lonely, make him reach out empty arms in his sleep. For Neil Bonner was only a man. When she first came into the store, he looked at her long, as a thirsty man may look at a flowing well. And she, with the heritage bequeathed her by Spike O'Brien, imagined daringly and smiled up into his eyes, not as the swart-skinned peoples should smile at the royal races, but as a woman smiles at a man. The thing was inevitable; only, he did not see it, and fought against her as fiercely and passionately as he was drawn toward her. And she? She was Jees Uck, by upbringing wholly and utterly a Toyaat Indian woman.

She came often to the post to trade. And often she sat by the big wood stove and chatted in broken English with Neil Bonner. And he came to look for her coming; and on the days she did not come he was worried and restless. Sometimes he stopped to think, and then she was met coldly, with a reserve that perplexed and piqued her, and which, she was convinced, was not sincere. But more often he did not dare to think, and then all went well

and there were smiles and laughter.   And
Amos Pentley, gasping like a stranded catfish,
his hollow cough a-reek with the grave, looked
upon it all and grinned.   He, who loved life,
could not live, and it rankled his soul that
others should be able to live.   Wherefore he
hated Bonner, who was so very much alive and
into whose eyes sprang joy at the sight of Jees
Uck.   As for Amos, the very thought of the
girl was sufficient to send his blood pounding
up into a hemorrhage.

Jees Uck, whose mind was simple, who
thought elementally and was unused to weighing life in its subtler quantities, read Amos
Pentley like a book.   She warned Bonner,
openly and bluntly, in few words ; but the
complexities of higher existence confused the
situation to him, and he laughed at her evident
anxiety.   To him, Amos was a poor, miserable
devil, tottering desperately into the grave.
And Bonner, who had suffered much, found it
easy to forgive greatly.

But one morning, during a bitter snap, he
got up from the breakfast table and went into

the store. Jees Uck was already there, rosy from the trail, to buy a sack of flour. A few minutes later, he was out in the snow lashing the flour on her sled. As he bent over he noticed a stiffness in his neck and felt a premonition of impending physical misfortune. And as he put the last half-hitch into the lashing and attempted to straighten up, a quick spasm seized him and he sank into the snow. Tense and quivering, head jerked back, limbs extended, back arched and mouth twisted and distorted, he appeared as though being racked limb from limb. Without cry or sound, Jees Uck was in the snow beside him; but he clutched both her wrists spasmodically, and as long as the convulsion endured she was helpless. In a few moments the spasm relaxed and he was left weak and fainting, his forehead beaded with sweat, his lips flecked with foam.

"Quick!" he muttered, in a strange, hoarse voice. "Quick! Inside!"

He started to crawl on hands and knees, but she raised him up, and, supported by her young arm, he made faster progress. As he entered the store the spasm seized him again, and his body writhed irresistibly away from her and rolled and curled on the floor. Amos Pentley came and looked on with curious eyes.

"Oh, Amos!" she cried in an agony of apprehension and helplessness, "him die, you think?" But Amos shrugged his shoulders and continued to look on.

Bonner's body went slack, the tense muscles easing down and an expression of relief coming into his face. "Quick!" he gritted between his teeth, his mouth twisting with the on-coming of the next spasm and with his effort to control it. "Quick, Jees Uck! The medicine! Never mind! Drag me!"

She knew where the medicine-chest stood, at the rear of the room, beyond the stove, and thither, by the legs, she dragged the struggling man. As the spasm passed, he began, very faint and very sick, to overhaul the chest. He had seen dogs die exhibiting symptoms similar to his own, and he knew what should be done. He held up a vial of chloral hydrate, but his fingers were too weak and nerveless to draw the cork. This Jees Uck did for him, while he was plunged into another convulsion. As he came out of it he found the open bottle proffered him and looked into the great black eyes of the woman and read what men have always read in the Mate-woman's eyes. Taking a full dose of the stuff, he sank back until another spasm had passed. Then he raised himself limply on his elbow.

"Listen, Jees Uck!" he said very slowly, as though aware of the necessity for haste and yet afraid to hasten. "Do what I say. Stay by my side, but do not touch me. I must be very quiet, but you must not go away." His jaw began to set and his face to quiver and distort with the forerunning pangs, but he gulped and struggled to master them. "Do not go away. And do not let Amos go away. Understand! Amos must stay right here."

She nodded her head, and he passed off into the first of many convulsions, which gradually diminished in force and frequency. Jees Uck hung over him, remembering his injunction and not daring to touch him. Once Amos

grew restless and made as though to go into
the kitchen; but a quick blaze from her eyes
quelled him, and after that, save for his labored
breathing and charnel cough, he was very
quiet.

Bonner slept. The blink of light that
marked the day disappeared. Amos, followed
about by the woman's eyes, lighted the kerosene lamps. Evening came on. Through the
north window the heavens were emblazoned
with an auroral display, which flamed and flared
and died down into blackness. Some time
after that, Neil Bonner roused. First he
looked to see that Amos was still there, then
smiled at Jees Uck and pulled himself up.
Every muscle was stiff and sore, and he smiled
ruefully, pressing and prodding himself as if to
ascertain the extent of the ravage. Then his
face went stern and businesslike.

"Jees Uck," he said, "take a candle. Go
into the kitchen. There is food on the table
— biscuits and beans and bacon; also, coffee
in the pot on the stove. Bring it here on the
counter. Also, bring tumblers and water and

whiskey, which you will find on the top shelf of the locker.   Do not forget the whiskey."

Having swallowed a stiff glass of the whiskey, he went carefully through the medicine chest, now and again putting aside, with definite purpose, certain bottles and vials.   Then he set to work on the food, attempting a crude analysis.   He had not been unused to the laboratory in his college days and was possessed of sufficient imagination to achieve results with his limited materials.   The condition of tetanus, which had marked his paroxysms, simplified matters, and he made but one test.   The coffee yielded nothing; nor did the beans. To the biscuits he devoted the utmost care. Amos, who knew nothing of chemistry, looked on with steady curiosity.   But Jees Uck, who had boundless faith in the white man's wisdom, and especially in Neil Bonner's wisdom, and who not only knew nothing but knew that she knew nothing, watched his face rather than his hands.

Step by step he eliminated possibilities, until he came to the final test.   He was using

a thin medicine vial for a tube, and this he
held between him and the light, watching the
slow precipitation of a salt through the solu-
tion contained in the tube.   He said nothing,
but he saw what he had expected to see.   And
Jees Uck, her eyes riveted on his face, saw
something, too, — something that made her
spring like a tigress upon Amos and with
splendid suppleness and strength bend his
body back across her knee.   Her knife was
out of its sheath and uplifted, glinting in the
lamplight.   Amos was snarling; but Bonner
intervened ere the blade could fall.

"That's a good girl, Jees Uck.   But never
mind.   Let him go!"

She dropped the man obediently, though
with protest writ large on her face; and his
body thudded to the floor.   Bonner nudged
him with his moccasined foot.

"Get up, Amos!" he commanded.   "You've
got to pack an outfit yet to-night and hit the
trail."

"You don't mean to say —" Amos blurted
savagely.

"I mean to say that you tried to kill me," Neil went on in cold, even tones. "I mean to say that you killed Birdsall, for all the company believes he killed himself. You used strychnine in my case. God knows with what you fixed him. Now I can't hang you. You're too near dead, as it is. But Twenty Mile is too small for the pair of us, and you've got to mush. It's two hundred miles to Holy Cross. You can make it if you're careful not to overexert. I'll give you grub, a sled, and three dogs. You'll be as safe as if you were in jail, for you can't get out of the country. And I'll give you one chance. You're almost dead. Very well. I shall send no word to the company until the spring. In the meantime, the thing for you to do is to die. Now, *mush!*"

"You go to bed!" Jees Uck insisted, when Amos had churned away into the night toward Holy Cross. "You sick man yet, Neil."

"And you're a good girl, Jees Uck," he answered. "And here's my hand on it. But you must go home."

"You don't like me," she said simply.

He smiled, helped her on with her *parka*, and led her to the door. "Only too well, Jees Uck," he said softly; "only too well."

After that the pall of the Arctic night fell deeper and blacker on the land. Neil Bonner discovered that he had failed to put proper valuation upon even the sullen face of the murderous and death-stricken Amos. It became very lonely at Twenty Mile. "For the love of God, Prentiss, send me a man," he wrote to the agent at Fort Hamilton, three hundred miles up river. Six weeks later the Indian messenger brought back a reply. It was characteristic: "Hell. Both feet frozen. Need him myself — Prentiss."

To make matters worse, most of the Toyaats were in the back country on the flanks of a caribou herd, and Jees Uck was with them. Removing to a distance seemed to bring her closer than ever, and Neil Bonner found himself picturing her, day by day, in camp and on trail. It is not good to be alone. Often he went out of the quiet store, bare-headed

and frantic, and shook his fist at the blink of
day that came over the southern sky-line.
And on still, cold nights he left his bed and
stumbled into the frost, where he assaulted the
silence at the top of his lungs, as though it
were some tangible, sentient thing that he
might arouse; or he shouted at the sleeping
dogs till they howled and howled again. One
shaggy brute he brought into the post, playing
that it was the new man sent by Prentiss. He
strove to make it sleep decently under blankets
at night and to sit at table and eat as a man
should; but the beast, mere domesticated wolf
that it was, rebelled, and sought out dark cor-
ners and snarled and bit him in the leg, and
was finally beaten and driven forth.

Then the trick of personification seized
upon Neil Bonner and mastered him. All the
forces of his environment metamorphosed into
living, breathing entities and came to live with
him. He re-created the primitive pantheon;
reared an altar to the sun and burned candle
fat and bacon grease thereon; and in the unfenced yard, by the long-legged caché, made a

frost devil, which he was wont to make faces
at and mock when the mercury oozed down
into the bulb.   All this in play, of course.
He said it to himself that it was in play, and
repeated it over and over to make sure, unaware that madness is ever prone to express
itself in make-believe and play.

One midwinter day, Father Champreau, a
Jesuit missionary, pulled into Twenty Mile.
Bonner fell upon him and dragged him into
the post, and clung to him and wept, until
the priest wept with him from sheer compas-
sion.   Then Bonner became madly hilarious
and made lavish entertainment, swearing val-
iantly that his guest should not depart.   But
Father Champreau was pressing to Salt Water
on urgent business for his order, and pulled
out next morning, with Bonner's blood threat-
ened on his head.

And the threat was in a fair way toward
realization, when the Toyaats returned from
their long hunt to the winter camp.   They
had many furs, and there was much trading
and stir at Twenty Mile.   Also, Jees Uck

came to buy beads and scarlet cloths and things, and Bonner began to find himself again. He fought for a week against her. Then the end came one night when she rose to leave. She had not forgotten her repulse, and the pride that drove Spike O'Brien on to complete the Northwest Passage by land was her pride.

"I go now," she said; "good night, Neil."

But he came up behind her. "Nay, it is not well," he said.

And as she turned her face toward his with a sudden joyful flash, he bent forward, slowly and gravely, as it were a sacred thing, and kissed her on the lips. The Toyaats had never taught her the meaning of a kiss upon the lips, but she understood and was glad.

With the coming of Jees Uck, at once things brightened up. She was regal in her happiness, a source of unending delight. The elemental workings of her mind and her naïve little ways made an immense sum of pleasurable surprise to the overcivilized man that had stooped to catch her up. Not alone was she

solace to his loneliness, but her primitiveness
rejuvenated his jaded mind.   It was as though,
after long wandering, he had returned to pil-
low his head in the lap of Mother Earth.
In short, in Jees Uck he found the youth of
the world — the youth and the strength and
the joy.

And to fill the full round of his need, and
that they might not see overmuch of each
other, there arrived at Twenty Mile one Sandy
MacPherson, as companionable a man as ever
whistled along the trail or raised a ballad by a
camp-fire.   A Jesuit priest had run into his
camp, a couple of hundred miles up the Yukon,
in the nick of time to say a last word over the
body of Sandy's partner.   And on departing,
the priest had said, " My son, you will be
lonely now."   And Sandy had bowed his
head brokenly.   " At Twenty Mile," the
priest added, " there is a lonely man.   You
have need of each other, my son."

So it was that Sandy became a welcome
third at the post, brother to the man and
woman that resided there.   He took Bonner

moose-hunting and wolf-trapping; and, in return, Bonner resurrected a battered and way-
worn volume and made him friends with
Shakespeare, till Sandy declaimed iambic pen-
tameters to his sled-dogs whenever they waxed
mutinous. And of the long evenings they
played cribbage and talked and disagreed about
the universe, the while Jees Uck rocked matronly in an easy-chair and darned their moccasins and socks.

Spring came. The sun shot up out of the
south. The land exchanged its austere robes
for the garb of a smiling wanton. Everywhere
light laughed and life invited. The days
stretched out their balmy length and the nights
passed from blinks of darkness to no darkness at all. The river bared its bosom, and
snorting steamboats challenged the wilderness.
There were stir and bustle, new faces, and fresh
facts. An assistant arrived at Twenty Mile,
and Sandy MacPherson wandered off with a
bunch of prospectors to invade the Koyokuk
country. And there were newspapers and
magazines and letters for Neil Bonner. And

Jees Uck looked on in worriment, for she knew his kindred talked with him across the world.

Without much shock, it came to him that his father was dead. There was a sweet letter of forgiveness, dictated in his last hours. There were official letters from the company, graciously ordering him to turn the post over to the assistant and permitting him to depart at his earliest pleasure. A long, legal affair from the lawyers informed him of interminable lists of stocks and bonds, real estate, rents, and chattels that were his by his father's will. And a dainty bit of stationery, sealed and monogrammed, implored dear Neil's return to his heart-broken and loving mother.

Neil Bonner did some swift thinking, and when the *Yukon Belle* coughed in to the bank on her way down to Bering Sea, he departed — departed with the ancient lie of quick return young and blithe on his lips.

" I'll come back, dear Jees Uck, before the first snow flies," he promised her, between the last kisses at the gang-plank.

And not only did he promise, but, like the majority of men under the same circumstances, he really meant it. To John Thompson, the new agent, he gave orders for the extension of unlimited credit to his wife, Jees Uck. Also, with his last look from the deck of the *Yukon Belle*, he saw a dozen men at work rearing the logs that were to make the most comfortable house along a thousand miles of river front — the house of Jees Uck, and likewise the house of Neil Bonner — ere the first flurry of snow. For he fully and fondly meant to come back. Jees Uck was dear to him, and, further, a golden future awaited the North. With his father's money he intended to verify that future. An ambitious dream allured him. With his four years of experience, and aided by the friendly coöperation of the P. C. Company, he would return to become the Rhodes of Alaska. And he would return, fast as steam could drive, as soon as he had put into shape the affairs of his father, whom he had never known, and comforted his mother, whom he had forgotten.

There was much ado when Neil Bonner came back from the Arctic. The fires were lighted and the fleshpots slung, and he took of it all and called it good. Not only was he bronzed and creased, but he was a new man under his skin, with a grip on things and a seriousness and control. His old companions were amazed when he declined to hit up the pace in the good old way, while his father's crony rubbed hands gleefully, and became an authority upon the reclamation of wayward and idle youth.

For four years Neil Bonner's mind had lain fallow. Little that was new had been added to it, but it had undergone a process of selection. It had, so to say, been purged of the trivial and superfluous. He had lived quick years, down in the world; and, up in the wilds, time had been given him to organize the confused mass of his experiences. His superficial standards had been flung to the winds and new standards erected on deeper and broader generalizations. Concerning civilization, he had gone away with one set of values,

had returned with another set of values.
Aided, also, by the earth smells in his nostrils
and the earth sights in his eyes, he laid hold
of the inner significance of civilization, be-
holding with clear vision its futilities and
powers. It was a simple little philosophy
he evolved. Clean living was the way to
grace. Duty performed was sanctification.
One must live clean and do his duty in order
that he might work. Work was salvation.
And to work toward life abundant, and more
abundant, was to be in line with the scheme
of things and the will of God.

Primarily, he was of the city. And his
fresh earth grip and virile conception of
humanity gave him a finer sense of civilization and endeared civilization to him. Day
by day the people of the city clung closer to
him and the world loomed more colossal.
And, day by day, Alaska grew more remote
and less real. And then he met Kitty Sharon
— a woman of his own flesh and blood and
kind; a woman who put her hand into his
hand and drew him to her, till he forgot the

day and hour and the time of the year the
first snow flies on the Yukon.

Jees Uck moved into her grand log-house
and dreamed away three golden summer
months. Then came the autumn, post-haste
before the down rush of winter. The air
grew thin and sharp, the days thin and
short. The river ran sluggishly, and skin
ice formed in the quiet eddies. All migra-
tory life departed south, and silence fell upon
the land. The first snow flurries came, and
the last homing steamboat bucked desperately into the running mush ice. Then came
the hard ice, solid cakes and sheets, till the
Yukon ran level with its banks. And
when all this ceased the river stood still
and the blinking days lost themselves in the
darkness.

John Thompson, the new agent, laughed;
but Jees Uck had faith in the mischances of
sea and river. Neil Bonner might be frozen
in anywhere between Chilkoot Pass and St.
Michael's, for the last travellers of the year
are always caught by the ice, when they ex-

change boat for sled and dash on through the long hours behind the flying dogs.

But no flying dogs came up the trail, nor down the trail, to Twenty Mile. And John Thompson told Jees Uck, with a certain gladness ill concealed, that Bonner would never come back again. Also, and brutally, he suggested his own eligibility. Jees Uck laughed in his face and went back to her grand log-house. But when midwinter came, when hope dies down and life is at its lowest ebb, Jees Uck found she had no credit at the store. This was Thompson's doing, and he rubbed his hands, and walked up and down, and came to his door and looked up at Jees Uck's house, and waited. And he continued to wait. She sold her dog-team to a party of miners and paid cash for her food. And when Thompson refused to honor even her coin, Toyaat Indians made her purchases, and sledded them up to her house in the dark.

In February the first post came in over the ice, and John Thompson read in the society column of a five months' old paper of the marriage of Neil Bonner and Kitty Sharon. Jees Uck held the door ajar and him outside while he imparted the information; and, when he had done, laughed pridefully and did not believe. In March, and all alone, she gave birth to a man-child, a brave bit of new life at which she marvelled. And at that hour, a year later, Neil Bonner sat by another bed, marvelling at another bit of new life that had fared into the world.

The snow went off the ground and the ice broke out of the Yukon. The sun journeyed north, and journeyed south again; and, the money from the dogs being spent, Jees Uck went back to her own people. Oche Ish, a shrewd hunter, proposed to kill the meat for her and her babe, and catch the salmon, if she would marry him. And Imego and Hah Yo and Wy Nooch, husky young hunters all, made similar proposals. But she elected to live alone and seek her own meat and fish. She sewed moccasins and *parkas* and mittens — warm, serviceable things, and pleasing to the eye, withal, what of the ornamental hair-tufts and bead work. These she sold to the miners, who were drifting faster into the land each year. And not only did she win food that was good and plentiful, but she laid money by, and one day took passage on the *Yukon Belle* down the river.

At St. Michael's she washed dishes in the kitchen of the post. The servants of the company wondered at the remarkable woman with the remarkable child, though they asked no questions and she vouchsafed nothing. But just before Bering Sea closed in for the year, she bought a passage south on a strayed sealing schooner. That winter she cooked for Captain Markheim's household at Unalaska, and in the spring continued south to Sitka on a whiskey sloop. Later, she appeared at Metlakahtla, which is near to St. Mary's on the end of the Pan-Handle, where she worked in the cannery through the salmon season. When autumn came and the Siwash fishermen prepared to return to Puget Sound, she embarked with a couple of families in a big cedar canoe; and with them she threaded the hazardous chaos of the Alaskan and Canadian coasts, till the Straits of Juan de Fuca were passed and she led her boy by the hand up the hard pave of Seattle.

There she met Sandy MacPherson, on a windy corner, very much surprised and, when he had heard her story, very wroth — not so wroth as he might have been, had he known of Kitty Sharon; but of her Jees Uck breathed no word, for she had never believed. Sandy, who read commonplace and sordid desertion into the circumstance, strove to dissuade her from her trip to San Francisco, where Neil Bonner was supposed to live when he was at home. And, having striven, he made her comfortable, bought her tickets and saw her off, the while smiling in her face and muttering "damshame" into his beard.

With roar and rumble, through daylight and dark, swaying and lurching between the dawns, soaring into the winter snows and sinking to summer valleys, skirting depths, leaping chasms, piercing mountains, Jees Uck and her boy were hurled south. But she had no fear of the iron stallion; nor was she stunned by this masterful civilization of Neil Bonner's people. It seemed, rather, that she saw with greater clearness the wonder that a man of such godlike race had held her in his arms. The screaming medley of San Francisco, with its restless shipping, belching factories, and thundering traffic, did not confuse her; instead, she comprehended swiftly the pitiful sordidness of Twenty Mile and the skin-lodged Toyaat village. And she looked down at the boy that clutched her hand and wondered that she had borne him by such a man.

She paid the hack-driver five prices and went up the stone steps to Neil Bonner's front door. A slant-eyed Japanese parleyed with her for a fruitless space, then led her inside and disappeared. She remained in the hall, which to her simple fancy seemed to be the guest room — the show-place wherein were arrayed all the household treasures with the frank purpose of parade and dazzlement. The walls and ceiling were of oiled and panelled redwood. The floor was more glassy

than glare ice, and she sought standing place
on one of the great skins that gave a sense
of security to the polished surface. A huge
fireplace — an extravagant fireplace, she deemed
it — yawned in the farther wall. A flood of
light, mellowed by stained glass, fell across
the room, and from the far end came the
white gleam of a marble figure.

This much she saw, and more, when the
slant-eyed servant led the way past another
room — of which she caught a fleeting glance
— and into a third, both of which dimmed
the brave show of the entrance hall. And to
her eyes the great house seemed to hold out
a promise of endless similar rooms. There
was such length and breadth to them, and
the ceilings were so far away! For the first
time since her advent into the white man's
civilization, a feeling of awe laid hold of her.
Neil, her Neil, lived in this house, breathed
the air of it, and lay down at night and slept!
It was beautiful, all this that she saw, and it
pleased her; but she felt, also, the wisdom
and mastery behind. It was the concrete

expression of power in terms of beauty, and it was the power that she unerringly divined.

And then came a woman, queenly tall, crowned with a glory of hair that was like a golden sun. She seemed to come toward Jees Uck as a ripple of music across still water; her sweeping garment itself a song, her body playing rhythmically beneath. Jees Uck was herself a man compeller. There were Oche Ish and Imego and Hah Yo and Wy Nooch, to say nothing of Neil Bonner and John Thompson and other white men that had looked upon her and felt her power. But she gazed upon the wide blue eyes and rose-white skin of this woman that advanced to meet her, and she measured her with woman's eyes looking through man's eyes; and as a man compeller she felt herself diminish and grow insignificant before this radiant and flashing creature.

"You wish to see my husband?" the woman asked; and Jees Uck gasped at the liquid silver of a voice that had never sounded harsh cries at snarling wolf dogs, nor moulded itself to a guttural speech, nor toughened in storm and frost and camp smoke.

"No," Jees Uck answered slowly and gropingly, in order that she might do justice to her English. "I come to see Neil Bonner."

"He is my husband," the woman laughed.

Then it was true! John Thompson had not lied that bleak February day, when she laughed pridefully and shut the door in his face. As once she had thrown Amos Pentley across her knee and ripped her knife into the air, so now she felt impelled to spring upon this woman and bear her back and down, and tear the life out of her fair body. But Jees Uck was thinking quickly and gave no sign, and Kitty Bonner little dreamed how intimately she had for an instant been related with sudden death.

Jees Uck nodded her head that she understood, and Kitty Bonner explained that Neil was expected at any moment. Then they sat down on ridiculously comfortable chairs, and Kitty sought to entertain her strange visitor, and Jees Uck strove to help her.

"You knew my husband in the North?" Kitty asked, once.

"Sure. I wash um clothes," Jees Uck had answered, her English abruptly beginning to grow atrocious.

"And this is your boy? I have a little girl."

Kitty caused her daughter to be brought, and while the children, after their manner, struck an acquaintance, the mothers indulged in the talk of mothers and drank tea from cups so fragile that Jees Uck feared lest hers should crumble to pieces between her fingers. Never had she seen such cups, so delicate and dainty. In her mind she compared them with the woman who poured the tea, and there uprose in contrast the gourds and pannikins of the Toyaat village and the clumsy mugs of Twenty Mile, to which she likened herself. And in such fashion and such terms the problem presented itself. She was beaten. There was a woman other than herself better fitted to bear and upbring Neil Bonner's children. Just as his people exceeded her people, so did his

womenkind exceed her.   They were the man
compellers, as their men were the world compellers. She looked at the rose-white tenderness
of Kitty Bonner's skin and remembered the
sun-beat on her own face.   Likewise she looked
from brown hand to white — the one, work-
worn and hardened by whip handle and paddle,
the other as guiltless of toil and soft as a new-
born babe's.   And, for all the obvious softness
and apparent weakness, Jees Uck looked into the
blue eyes and saw the mastery she had seen in
Neil Bonner's eyes and in the eyes of Neil
Bonner's people.

"Why, it's Jees Uck!" Neil Bonner said,
when he entered.   He said it calmly, with even
a ring of joyful cordiality, coming over to her
and shaking both her hands, but looking into
her eyes with a worry in his own that she
understood.

"Hello, Neil!" she said.   "You look
much good."

"Fine, fine, Jees Uck," he answered
heartily, though secretly studying Kitty for
some sign of what had passed between the two.

Yet he knew his wife too well to expect, even though the worst had passed, such a sign.

"Well, I can't say how glad I am to see you," he went on. "What's happened? Did you strike a mine? And when did you get in?"

"Oo-a, I get in to-day," she replied, her voice instinctively seeking its guttural parts. "I no strike it, Neil. You know Cap'n Markheim, Unalaska? I cook, his house, long time. No spend money. Bime-by, plenty. Pretty good, I think, go down and see White Man's Land. Very fine, White Man's Land, very fine," she added. Her English puzzled him, for Sandy and he had sought, constantly, to better her speech, and she had proved an apt pupil. Now it seemed that she had sunk back into her race. Her face was guileless, stolidly guileless, giving no cue. Kitty's untroubled brow likewise baffled him. What had happened? How much had been said? and how much guessed?

While he wrestled with these questions and

while Jees Uck wrestled with her problem —
never had he looked so wonderful and great —
a silence fell.

"To think that you knew my husband in
Alaska!" Kitty said softly.

Knew him! Jees Uck could not forbear a
glance at the boy she had borne him, and his
eyes followed hers mechanically to the window
where played the two children. An iron band
seemed to tighten across his forehead. His
knees went weak and his heart leaped up and
pounded like a fist against his breast. His
boy! He had never dreamed it!

Little Kitty Bonner, fairylike in gauzy lawn,
with pinkest of cheeks and bluest of dancing
eyes, arms outstretched and lips puckered in
invitation, was striving to kiss the boy. And
the boy, lean and lithe, sunbeaten and browned,
skin-clad and in hair-fringed and hair-tufted
muclucs that showed the wear of the sea and
rough work, coolly withstood her advances,
his body straight and stiff with the peculiar
erectness common to children of savage people.
A stranger in a strange land, unabashed and

unafraid, he appeared more like an untamed animal, silent and watchful, his black eyes flashing from face to face, quiet so long as quiet endured, but prepared to spring and fight and tear and scratch for life, at the first sign of danger.

The contrast between boy and girl was striking, but not pitiful. There was too much strength in the boy for that, waif that he was of the generations of Shpack, Spike O'Brien, and Bonner. In his features, clean cut as a cameo and almost classic in their severity, there were the power and achievement of his father, and his grandfather, and the one known as the Big Fat, who was captured by the Sea People and escaped to Kamchatka.

Neil Bonner fought his emotion down, swallowed it down, and choked over it, though his face smiled with good humor and the joy with which one meets a friend.

"Your boy, eh, Jees Uck?" he said. And then turning to Kitty: "Handsome fellow! He'll do something with those two hands of his in this our world."

Kitty nodded concurrence. " What is your name ? " she asked.

The young savage flashed his quick eyes upon her and dwelt over her for a space, seeking out, as it were, the motive beneath the question.

" Neil," he answered deliberately when the scrutiny had satisfied him.

" Injun talk," Jees Uck interposed, glibly manufacturing languages on the spur of the moment. " Him Injun talk, *nee-al*, all the same ' cracker.' Him baby, him like cracker ; him cry for cracker. Him say, ' *Nee-al, nee-al*,' all time him say, ' *Nee-al*.' Then I say that um name. So um name all time Nee-al."

Never did sound more blessed fall upon Neil Bonner's ear than that lie from Jees Uck's lips. It was the cue, and he knew there was reason for Kitty's untroubled brow.

" And his father ? " Kitty asked. " He must be a fine man."

" Oo-a, yes," was the reply. " Um father fine man. Sure ! "

" Did you know him, Neil ? " queried Kitty.

" Know him ?   Most intimately," Neil answered, and harked back to dreary Twenty Mile and the man alone in the silence with his thoughts.

And here might well end the story of Jees Uck, but for the crown she put upon her renunciation.   When she returned to the North to dwell in her grand log-house, John Thompson found that the P. C. Company could make a shift somehow to carry on its business without his aid.   Also, the new agent and the succeeding agents received instructions that the woman Jees Uck should be given whatsoever goods and grub she desired, in whatsoever quantities she ordered, and that no charge should be placed upon the books.   Further, the company paid yearly to the woman Jees Uck a pension of five thousand dollars.

When he had attained suitable age, Father Champreau laid hands upon the boy, and the time was not long when Jees Uck received letters regularly from the Jesuit college in Maryland.   Later on these letters came from Italy, and still later from France.   And in the end there returned to Alaska one Father Neil, a man mighty for good in the land, who loved his mother and who ultimately went into a wider field and rose to high authority in the order.

Jees Uck was a young woman when she went back into the North, and men still looked upon her and yearned. But she lived straight, and no breath was ever raised save in commendation. She stayed for a while with the good sisters at Holy Cross, where she learned to read and write and became versed in practical medicine and surgery. After that she returned to her grand log-house and gathered about her the young girls of the Toyaat village, to show them the way of their feet in the world. It is neither Protestant nor Catholic, this school in the house built by Neil Bonner for Jees Uck, his wife; but the missionaries of all the sects look upon it with equal favor. The latch-string is always out, and tired prospectors and trail-weary men turn aside from the flowing river or frozen trail to rest there for a space and be warm by her fire. And, down in the

States, Kitty Bonner is pleased at the interest her husband takes in Alaskan education and the large sums he devotes to that purpose; and, though she often smiles and chaffs, deep down and secretly she is but the prouder of him.

WORKS BY JACK LONDON

THE SEA-WOLF

With illustrations by W. J. AYLWARD

"'The Sea-Wolf,' Jack London's latest novel of adventure, is one that every reader with good red blood in his veins will hail with delight. There is no fumbling of the trigger here, no nervous and uncertain sighting along the barrel, but the quick decisive aim and the bull's-eye every time." — *Mail and Express*, New York.

"Jack London's 'The Sea-Wolf' is marvellously truthful. . . . Reading it through at a sitting, we have found it poignantly interesting . . . a superb piece of craftsmanship." — *The New York Tribune*.

"Exciting, original, fascinating. . . . Novel and pleasing. . . . So original, vivid, and daring that it commands attention." — *Chicago Record-Herald*.

THE CALL OF THE WILD

With illustrations by PHILIP R. GOODWIN and CHARLES LIVINGSTON BULL

Decorated by CHARLES EDWARD HOOPER

"A big story in sober English and with thorough art in the construction; a wonderfully perfect bit of work; a book that will be heard of. The dog's adventures are as exciting as any man's exploits could be, and Mr. London's workmanship is wholly satisfying." — *The New York Sun*.

"Even the most listless reader will be stirred by the virile force of the story, the strong, sweeping strokes with which the pictures of the northern wilds and the life therein are painted by the narrator, and the insight given into the soul of the primitive in nature. . . . More than that, it is one of the very best stories of the year, and one that will not be forgotten." — *The Plain Dealer*, Cleveland.

"The story is one that will stir the blood of every lover of a life in its closest relation to nature. Whoever loves the open or adventure for its own sake will find 'The Call of the Wild' a most fascinating book." — *The Brooklyn Eagle*.

WORKS BY JACK LONDON

THE FAITH OF MEN
And Other Stories

"Mr. London's art as a story-teller nowhere manifests itself more strongly than in the swift, dramatic close of his stories. There is no hesitancy or uncertainty of touch. From the start the story moves straight to the inevitable conclusion." — *Courier-Journal.*

THE CHILDREN OF THE FROST

"Told with something of that same vigorous and honest manliness and indifference with which Mr. Kipling makes unbegging yet direct and unfailing appeal to the sympathy of his reader."
—*Richmond Dispatch.*

THE PEOPLE OF THE ABYSS
With many illustrations from photographs

"Mr. London's book is a powerful presentation of a repellent theme, but it is well that thinking men should know the facts about these horrors — hunger and filth and cold and suffering — that they may set to work to change a system that works such an iniquity."
— *Nashville News.*

THE KEMPTON-WACE LETTERS
By JACK LONDON and ANNA STRUNSKY

"I am much impressed by the book . . . it is an entertaining, thought-compelling work. I should not be surprised if it became a classic on the subject of love."
— EDWIN MARKHAM, Westerleigh, Staten Island, N.Y.